"Look, Fury," Russ began. "If it was just your flaky, irresponsible behavior I had to overlook, I could live with it. I'm used to it by now. But there's a limit to my understanding, patience, and most important, my money. I'm not renting rooms for free, you know. Maybe your parents or someone could wire you some money."

A hurt expression swept swiftly across Fury's face. Fury was sure that Russ knew that he didn't have any parents and that he'd grown up in foster homes. He had mentioned it to him a couple of weeks after he had moved in.

Russ looked embarrassed. "I'm sorry I said that. I forgot about your family situation," he apologized. "But what I'm getting at is that your rent's more than two weeks overdue. You have to admit that I've waited long enough for you to pay up. And now Leslie just told me that you quit your job."

Fury looked with disappointment at Leslie, who lowered her eyes, unable to look him in the face. Without having to say a single word, her downcast eyes told Fury exactly how she felt. "I'm sorry, too," they told him. "I'm sorry I had to fink on you."

"Les and I have talked things over and we both agree that when Pamela gets back tomorrow morning, we need to hold a meeting to discuss some house problems. In the meantime, I want you to shape up."

Other books in the **ENDLESS SUMMER** series:

#1: Treading Water
#2: Too Hot To Handle

ENDLESS *Summer*

ON THE EDGE
Linda Davidson

IVY BOOKS • NEW YORK

Ivy Books
Published by Ballantine Books

Produced by Butterfield Press, Inc.
133 Fifth Avenue
New York, New York 10003

Library of Congress Catalog Card Number: 88-91136

ISBN 0-8041-0243-0

Printed in Canada

First Edition: October 1988

This one is for
all the Goldsteins:
Phyllis, Gary, Dorothy,
Jessica, and Helane,
and my beloved Parents,
Murray and Theodora

Chapter 1

"Fury, I'm leaving. If you want a ride to the beach, you'd better move it!" Leslie Stevens shouted into the den as she did every morning on her way out to the carport.

Angelo DeFurie, better known as Fury, barely heard her over the noise of the hair dryer he had borrowed a week ago from his girl friend, Tracy Berberian, and had conveniently forgotten to return. Fury continued blow-drying his half–platinum blond, half-pink hair.

He had just finished coloring the top part of his hair. The urge to change his hair color hadn't been a sudden one. Fury had felt it coming for several weeks, but up until now he'd been too chicken to do it. Around dawn this morning, however, he had awakened from a restless sleep

1

and had tiptoed out of the den and into the downstairs bathroom with the coloring kit in hand.

It wasn't a real peroxide job like the rest of his bleached-blond hair, just a cellophane rinse that would wash out in a week or two—right around the time he'd be sick of having pink hair. Right now he was concentrating on spiking the front with gel, and he wasn't about to rush just so that Leslie could get to work on time. So what if they were late? The nine-to-five routine was quickly becoming old hat.

Leslie stuck her head back in the door and screamed, "Fury, I'm leaving." Fury switched off the hair dryer and turned toward her. Leslie gasped. "What did you do to your hair?"

"I dyed it to match my sneakers. Like it?"

Fury got a kick out of watching Leslie's pretty face light up in surprise as her big, blue eyes traveled from his bright pink hair down to his bright pink high-tops.

"They match all right. Just out of curiosity, what happened to your purple ones? No, don't tell me. You traded them to a guy with purple hair."

"Leslie, you're amazing. How'd you know?"

"The boy with green hair told me," she answered.

"You saw a boy with green hair? What shade green? You know, I was just thinking about dying my hair green—after the pink washes out, of course," Fury explained.

"I was just kidding. *The Boy With Green Hair* is the name of an old movie."

"Is it out on video? I've got to see it."

"I don't know. But would you like to see a scene from *The Boy With Pink Hair*? Watch as two young lifeguards lose their jobs because one of them can't finish drying his hair in time to go to work. . . . Fury, we have to go. Are you coming now or not?"

"I'm coming, I'm coming. I just have to put my earrings in." Fury inserted one rhinestone stud after the other in his left ear, then started on his right.

Fury, I don't have all day to wait for you to put on your jewelry!" Leslie protested.

Fury could tell that Leslie was getting irritated, so instead of making her late he said, "Go on without me. I'll catch a ride with Tracy."

"Then *you'll* be late, and Jeff will be on your back," Leslie reminded him.

"Chill out, Leslie. I can handle his heat better than you can."

In truth, Fury didn't care whether Jeff, the senior lifeguard at Marina Bay Beach, was upset with him or not. Being a relief lifeguard hadn't exactly been Fury's idea of how to spend the summer. He had come up to Marina Bay when the fog had rolled into San Francisco Bay in late June. Since the fog blanketed the entire area—and especially the beaches—every morning, Fury had decided to split the city by the bay and head south. In Marina Bay, the water was much milder, and Fury had fully intended to spend the entire summer surfing.

And that's what he would have been doing this morning if Jeff hadn't come up with the brilliant idea of hiring him after Fury had saved Alex from drowning. Alex was the seven-year-old kid that Jed, one of Fury's housemates, was baby-sitting for the summer. Everyone in the beach house, with the exception of Tracy and Pamela, had somehow gotten involved in Alex's near-fatal accident. Leslie, who had had that particular morning off, had offered to give Jed a windsurfing lesson. Jed, who hadn't had the morning off, nevertheless hadn't wanted to miss the chance to improve his windsurfing skills— or the opportunity to spend time alone with Leslie. Jed had asked Russ, Leslie's brother, to look after Alex for him that morning. Russ had planned to take Alex fishing off the pier. But he had left Alex alone for a minute, and the kid had run off down the pier and had fallen into the water and almost drowned. Fortunately, Fury and his buddies, Nick and Danny, had been surfing nearby, and they had witnessed the fall. Fury had saved Alex's life—and for his heroic efforts, he had somehow managed to mess up his own life.

After the rescue, Jeff had offered him the job of relief lifeguard, and Fury had been thrilled. He needed the money, and with everyone telling him what a hero he was, it was easy to accept the position. What he wouldn't give now to have just said no to Jeff and not taken the boring job!

"Seriously, Les, go ahead. I'll catch up with you," Fury told her.

"Okay then, see you later!" Leslie called out, storming out of the den. Fury heard the door of the house slam hard behind her. In spite of his attempt not to make her late, he was sure she was angry with him anyway for putting her in a no-win situation. If she waited for him, she'd be late. If she didn't, he'd be late and behind in his schedule. And that meant he wouldn't be relieving her from her lifeguard station until close to noon, depending upon when Tracy was due at T-Shirts for Two, the T-shirt and poster shop in town where she worked.

He finished putting the back on his last earring and decided to return Tracy's hair dryer. He hated to admit it, but Leslie had gotten to him; he really *didn't* want to be late. He felt annoyed at himself now for not making an effort to hurry and go with her. He hoped that Tracy was already up and ready to leave. In any case, he was happy to have an excuse to go up to her room: she always looked so fresh and beautiful early in the morning, when most people Fury knew looked their worst—including himself.

Before going upstairs, Fury looked into the mirror one last time to make sure he looked okay. He liked the way his pink hair stood on end in the front, and was pretty sure Tracy would like it, too. He unplugged the hair dryer;

then, holding it like a gun; he swaggered out of the den.

"Bang, bang," he joked to Russell Stevens, Leslie's six-foot-tall brother, as he stepped out of the bathroom and into Fury's path.

"Not so fast on the draw—Pinky," Russ shot back. "Where do you think you're going?"

"To see if Tracy's up," Fury answered.

"She's in the upstairs bathroom. Which is why *I'm* in the downstairs bathroom. Hey, are you at all aware of the mess you made in here?" Russ asked, pointing inside the bathroom. "I almost had a heart attack just now. There are these dark red blotches that look exactly like blood all over the sink and floor—not to mention my mother's expensive towels. Luckily, I saw the coloring kit lying on the floor, so I figured you hadn't cut yourself shaving and bled to death."

"Don't worry, Russ. That stuff washes out," Fury explained.

"Oh, and I suppose that makes dyeing the entire bathroom pink all right."

"I didn't say that. I was planning on cleaning up after I finished drying my hair. I just forgot."

"Well, maybe you should write yourself a little note, like 'Remember to clean up after myself around the house.' Which reminds me—I'm going to write myself a little reminder to yell at Leslie when she gets home. If she hadn't been such a flake, I wouldn't have to put up with you and your mess all summer," Russ said angrily.

Fury didn't have to ask what Russ meant by

Leslie being such a flake. He knew that Russ thought Leslie had really blown it when she rented out the den to Fury for the summer without discussing it with him first. Right after his parents had left for a summer-long vacation in Europe, Russ had cracked up his sister's brand new Suzuki. He had rented out all the other rooms in the house himself to come up with the money to fix the car. Not that he had done such a hot job of it, Fury thought.

Pamela Easton, the Princess, as Fury called her, had moved into the beach house the day after he had along with her eight pieces of matching Gucci luggage. Fury knew the exact number of bags she owned because he and Russ had carried all of them up to the master suite. Then, a few weeks later, after spending most of her time sunning herself on the deck outside her bedroom, Pamela had taken off. Fury had no idea when she was planning to return. In the meantime, he supposed that the master bedroom was as good a place as any for her to store her suitcases.

Fury thought chubby Jed Mason, who shared Russ's room, was a nice enough nerd. He had more than his share of brains, but in the looks department, the girls didn't think Jed was so hot. In fact, Jed had this terrific knack for turning off the opposite sex. Leslie, Fury had observed, seemed to like him as a friend, but nothing more. She didn't seem to mind giving him a windsurfing lesson every now and then.

Fury had a hunch that in spite of the fact that Leslie was going out with Jeff, Jed still had a crush on her. Fury also suspected nothing would come of it. Jed was just no competition for Jeff. Although he tried hard enough, especially when Leslie was teaching him, and read up on every sport, Jed would never be a jock—at least not the way Jeff, head lifeguard at Marina Bay Beach was.

Russ looked down at the hair dryer in Fury's hand. "So, if you're finished fixing your 'do, maybe you could start cleaning up the bathroom now," he suggested.

Fury put one foot on the stairs. "I'll get to it as soon as I return Tracy's hair dryer," he said.

Just then Jed came bouncing down the stairs. "Your hair looks cool," he said to Fury as he walked past him and headed for the kitchen.

At least Jed was friendly and not always on his back like Russ, Fury though as he slowly continued to make his way upstairs, trying to casually edge away from Russ.

"I guess I won't hold my breath waiting for you to clean up!" Russ yelled after him. "Tell Tracy to hurry up so I can use the upstairs bathroom!"

Fury knocked on Tracy's door. "Trace! Can I come in?"

"Sure," she answered. "I'm decent."

"The bathroom's all yours," Fury called down to Russ. He walked into Tracy's bedroom. "I'm returning your hair dryer. Sorry I kept it so long." He set it down on the dresser by the door.

"Oh, thanks. I've been looking all over for it. If I don't dry my hair right after I wash it, it gets pretty unruly." Tracy's black hair hung down wildly over her face as she leaned over to pull on her fancy white cowboy boots.

She stood up and threw her hair back over her shoulders. The blood that had rushed to her head while it had hung upside down had brought a lot of color to her cheeks and lips. Fury thought she looked even more fiery and exotic than usual. He couldn't help but think how he would like to take her by surprise and just walk up to her and kiss her.

"Aah!" she shrieked, as soon her hair was away from her eyes and she could see Fury clearly.

Fury figured that Tracy didn't have to be a mind reader to know what he was thinking. His urge to kiss her was written all over his face. And now it was equally obvious to Fury that Tracy, too, wanted to kid around. Pretending that the scream had fueled his passion, he brushed the top of his hair, careful not to disturb the spikes, wrapped an imaginary cape around him, and dramatically strutted toward her. Her brown eyes widened and she crossed her fingers as if she were fending off a vampire.

"Back, back!" I'm being attacked by a creature from the Pink Lagoon," she called out.

"Throw back your throat. I vant to kiss you,"

Fury said with a Count Dracula accent, coming closer.

But when he swooped her up in his arms, drew her toward him, and was about to kiss her on the neck vampire style, Tracy ended the game with a serious, warm, wet kiss on the lips. Fury responded by kissing her back passionately. He stroked her wild hair.

"Fury, whatever possessed you?" Tracy had a chance to ask when their lips finally parted.

Fury dropped the Count Dracula accent and said in a normal voice, "I don't now. I just like kissing you, especially when you make a game of it. I just can't resist those inviting, ruby red lips, that just-brushed, jet-black hair, that fresh, out-of-the-shower smell about you first thing in the morning. Besides, since when do I need a reason to want to kiss you? Isn't loving you enough?"

The game might have been over, but the fun was just beginning, Fury thought, about to kiss her again.

But Tracy pulled away and said, "I wasn't talking about the kiss, silly. I was referring to your hair."

"Oh, my hair. I thought you were just playing around to get me to kiss you. Weren't you?"

"Well, not really." Tracy shrugged. "At first I was just reacting to your new hair color. Then, when I realized you wanted to play around, I decided to go along with the game."

"Wait a second. Let me get this straight. Are

you telling me now that you don't like my hair? C'mon, Tracy, I know you love it. Tell me you love it." He just couldn't believe that she didn't.

But Tracy quickly set him straight. "I don't want to hurt your feelings, Fury, but I liked it better when it was all platinum blond. I think the pink hair sticking up in the front is pretty funny looking. But, don't worry, sweetheart. Looks aren't everything."

"What's that supposed to mean? Do you really hate my hair?" Fury asked.

"Yeah, pretty much. But I still love *you*. And maybe it'll grow on me the way you did. Just in case it doesn't, is there any chance you could wash it out in the next few days?"

In spite of Tracy's attempt to humor him, Fury felt too dejected to answer. He couldn't care less about what Russ and Leslie had thought of his looks, but Tracy's opinion really mattered to him. "Thanks for your support, Tracy. You know, I really thought you would like this."

"Well, if you were so concerned about me liking it," Tracy countered, "why didn't you tell me what you were planning to do first?"

"I wanted to surprise you," Fury argued.

"Well, you surprised me all right. Look, there's no sense in arguing about it now. What's done is done. I'm already getting used to it. Can I give you a ride to work?" Tracy asked nicely, as if trying to make amends.

"Nah. I'll skate in," Fury told her. "I'm sure you wouldn't want to be seen with me, anyway."

"Fine. Be that way!" Tracy answered. "If that's how you feel."

"Yeah. That's how I feel." Fury walked out of the room, frowning. If Tracy wanted to act so unfriendly, it was her business. Maybe she had gotten up on the wrong side of the bed. It was just as well. Riding into town on the back of her Honda motorcycle probably would have destroyed his hair.

Chapter 2

Fury came downstairs to straighten up the bathroom with a little less swagger in his walk. So far this morning nothing had gone right. With the exception of Jed, everyone in the house hated his hair, and worse yet, they were all mad at him. But cleaning up the bathroom could wait a few minutes, he decided. He walked into the dining room where Jed was eating breakfast. If anyone could cheer him up, he could.

"What's up besides your hair?" Jed asked, friendly as always.

"Not much." Fury pulled a chair out from under the dining room table and slouched into it.

"Your hair's pink, but the rest of you doesn't seem to be. What's the deal?"

13

"Nobody digs the new color," Fury complained.

"What do they know? Your hair's where it's at. It's in. It's icy. It's fresh. It's rad. It's—"

"Hey, man, slow down. It's not red, it's pink," Fury pointed out.

"I didn't say red, I said rad. You know, short for radical," Jed explained.

"Oh, rad, yeah. I hear you, Jed. But I know you're only saying it to make me feel good."

"No I'm not. I really like it. It's really you. The point is, do you like it?" Jed took a bite of toast.

"Of course I do. It's totally hip."

"Then that's all that matters. Besides, you're entitled to make your own personal fashion statement. It's your hair, and you can do whatever you want with it."

"Hey, man. You're right. Thanks a lot. I feel better already."

"No problem," Jed said. He sipped his coffee. "Have you had breakfast yet?"

"Nah, but I don't have time. I've got to get to work and I still have to clean up the bathroom before I go. I'll pick up something to eat on the way. I guess I'd better get a move on," Fury said.

"It's too bad you have to take off," Jed said.

"You're telling me! Working for a living is not all it's cracked up to be."

"No kidding. Hey, let's talk again sometime."

"Sure thing." Fury stood up and, feeling better about his hair and about himself in general, walked into the bathroom. The bright morning sun filtered through the opaque glass window. Anxious to get out of the house and feel the sun's full warmth, Fury quickly scrubbed the dirty sink and floor. Then he grabbed the stained, beige towels from the rack and used them to dry the floor. When he was done, he threw the towels and some laundry detergent into the washing machine in the utility closet in the hallway. After turning on the machine, he made tracks to the den to pick up his skateboard, his shades, and his Walkman.

Just before heading out for the day, Fury stopped in the dining room. "Jed, could you do me a favor? Will you be around for a half hour or so?"

"Sure. What is it?" Jed asked.

"I've got to leave for work. When the washing machine stops, could you throw those towels into the dryer?"

"Yeah. I've got to leave in about forty-five minutes, so it should be done before then."

"Thanks. I owe you one. See you later," Fury said, heading for the front door. "Have fun with Alex!" he called just as the door shut.

Once outside, he set down his skateboard, put on his shades and his earphones, slipped his Walkman in the back pocket of his red lifeguard shorts, and hopped on his board. Jumping the front steps, he thought about Jed. In spite of the fact that they didn't have all that much in common, Fury could really rap with him. It just could be, Fury thought as he landed on the walkway, that he had Jed all wrong. Maybe the brain from Berkeley had more going for him than Fury had originally thought. He certainly couldn't forget the fact that earlier in the summer Jed had convinced Russ not to throw Fury out of the house when he couldn't pay his rent on time. Jed had even gone so far as to lay out the rent money for him until Fury received his first paycheck.

When Fury reached the street, he hopped the curb and started focusing on his skateboarding. He had to pump his board to get going on the flat section of Sandpiper, and then carefully weave his way around oncoming cars, jumping quickly on and off the sidewalk. On the gradual downhill section of the street he crouched down on his board to pick up speed.

Sandpiper eventually butted into a paved bicycle path that paralleled the beach and the main highway that led into Marina Bay. Not having to look out for oncoming traffic on this stretch, Fury could be more laid back on his board and listen to music on his Walkman. He turned it on without stopping and skated down the path to a hot tune.

Fury loved to take this route when he had the time. Besides being a dream to skate on, the smooth, asphalt strip snaked its way past a public par course and putting green. On a Saturday or Sunday, or any day when he wasn't in a rush, he liked to hop off his skateboard and fool around on the balance beam, do a couple of chin-ups, or go hand over hand on the parallel bars. But this Thursday morning, already an hour late to work, he didn't even have time to watch a group of elderly golfers chip and putt their way to the ninth hole on the green.

Late to work or not, he couldn't resist doing some end overs and kick turns where the bike strip opened into a large, asphalt circle to accommodate a public drinking fountain. He did a grind on the water-fountain step and took off again down the bike path. Passing an overflowing litter can, he ollied over a stray soda can. He watched his pink high-tops make a perfect landing back on his board. He was in great form. At the moment there wasn't a cloud in the sky or a worrisome thought in his head. The bright, morning sun warmed his lean body through his turquoise T-shirt; the last thing on his mind was getting to work.

The bike path ended at the self-service gas station and minimart at the edge of town. Here the asphalt strip became paved sidewalk and part of Surfrider—Marina Bay's main drag, where skateboards weren't allowed. Even though Fury knew the law, he kept on going until he saw a police car cruise up Surfrider. He quickly slid to a stop, turned off his Walkman, and slid his earphones down around his neck. He picked up his board, and started walking the rest of the way into town.

Just before passing the store where Tracy worked, T-Shirts For Two, he stopped by a parked car, put his board down, and took a comb out of his back pocket. He looked in the car's side-view mirror and saw that he didn't need to comb his hair. The pink spikes that had been temporarily flattened by the metal band of the headset had sprung back into place on their own.

He was about to walk into T-Shirts For Two when he caught himself. He wasn't about to give Tracy a break by stopping in and saying hello as he did every morning. Although he knew he'd miss seeing and talking to her and he hated to be on the outs with her, he was determined this time to wait until *she* apologized to *him*.

And he was sure she would. Fury was well aware that they shared more than just a strong physical attraction toward each other. They both played guitar and liked spending their evenings jamming together. Fury often acted as Tracy's audience and her backup bass as she worked up a new country-western song. Tracy's next appearance, in the Nashville Night show at the Surfrider Cafe and Restaurant, was coming up soon, and she still needed a lot of practice. So, Fury thought, she was bound to make up with him before the day was over.

He stepped on the end of his board, kicked it into the air, and caught it with one hand. Pleased with his stunt and his decision not to stop in and see Tracy, he sauntered down the street to get some breakfast. His good mood fizzled, however, once he stepped inside the Surfrider Cafe.

"Well, what a surprise!" Jeff said as he approached Fury while carrying a container of coffee to go. "Good morning. Any chance of you coming to work today? Some of us are already on our coffee break. Others are waiting for *you* so they can take theirs."

"I'm on my way over to relieve Leslie right now. I was just getting a cup of coffee and a pastry to bring with me," Fury replied. Actually, the midmorning air was so warm and still, he had sort of planned on sitting down at a table outside to have his breakfast—before he ran into his boss, that was.

"Then I won't detain you a minute longer," Jeff said, smiling. He strolled out of the cafe with his coffee.

Fury couldn't miss the sarcastic edge to Jeff's voice, and he added Jeff's name to the ever-growing list of people he had managed to bend out of shape that morning.

Fury walked over to the take-out counter and ordered his breakfast. *At least Jeff didn't make a nasty comment about my hair*, Fury thought as he waited for his order. Maybe he even liked it, but he was too annoyed with Fury to pay him a compliment. *No*, Fury said to himself, reconsidering. *The punk look's definitely not Jeff's style*. The senior lifeguard wore his blond hair short, almost in a crew cut.

Fury paid the man at the counter, picked up his coffee and apple turnover, and headed out of the cafe.

As he plodded across the sand to Leslie's lifeguard station, Fury could have easily let himself be further distracted by all kinds of beach activities: two-man volleyball and paddleball games, Frisbees and kites flying, noisy naked toddlers playing with sand toys or collecting seashells by the water's edge, and older girls in skimpy bikinis sunning themselves on big beach towels and doing nothing.

There was also all the board, body, and windsurfing action in the water. And he could have also got caught up for an hour or two just watching guys his own age having water fights or filling up balloons with water to throw them at their girl friends or at each other. But he concentrated on getting to his post, and he arrived at Tower Four just in time to see Jeff disappearing down the beach.

"I'm here," Fury called up to Leslie.

Leslie looked at her Swatch, then down at Fury. "I didn't expect you so early."

Fury couldn't tell whether she was being serious or sarcastic. "What time is it, anyway?"

"Eleven o'clock," she answered gruffly.

"Oh. I didn't realize it was that late," Fury said. Actually, if he had thought about it, there was no way he could have been any earlier. But being timely just wasn't his number-one priority this morning—the sun was. "Sorry, Les. I got hung up cleaning the bathroom."

"You don't have to bother to apologize to me," Leslie said as she climbed down. "I'm not your boss. Jeff's the one who's on the verge of firing you."

"How do you know?" Fury asked, startled.

"He just told me. He also asked me to tell you that if you're late one more time or if you break the rules again, he's handing you your walking papers."

"Why didn't he tell me himself?"

"How should I know? Why don't you ask him yourself?" Leslie countered.

"I think I will. You'd better take your break now, though. It is getting late."

"Tell me about it. By the time I get back it'll be time for me to leave for lunch," Leslie said as Fury shoved his skateboard under her lifeguard chair, then climbed up to take his place in it.

"You might as well not come back until after lunch," Fury advised her. "I'll skip mine, since I'm only up to breakfast so far."

Leslie smiled up at Fury. "Thanks. That sounds great. Can you please pass me down my beach bag?"

Fury handed it to her, then smiled back at her. It felt good to do something right for a change. He removed his container of coffee from the paper sack, took off the lid, and took a small sip. The hot coffee tasted good to him.

"Got any messages for Tracy? I think I'll stop by and see if she wants to have lunch with me," Leslie informed Fury.

"No thanks." Being nice to Leslie was one thing; being nice to Tracy so soon after she had insulted him was another. "Catch you later."

Chapter 3

Fury set his coffee down on the platform, then reached inside the paper sack for his apple turnover. He wolfed down the whole pastry in five big bites. Still hungry, he picked up his container of coffee and drained it. The hot beverage took the edge off his appetite, but he wondered if it had been such a good idea to give up his lunch hour. No point in worrying about it now, he decided, especially when he had more important things on his mind like the thought that Jeff might fire him.

Well, what if he did? Fury had pretty much had it with the boring job, anyway. To tell the truth, he didn't know how many more days he could stomach sitting in a lifeguard's chair watching everyone around him having fun in the sun. Without a lunch break, the only break he'd get today was when he changed chairs. Then he could listen to tunes on his Walkman as he bopped over to the next lifeguard station. Big thrill! Compared with that, playing musical chairs even seemed exciting.

Just the thought of having to sit still all day made him feel even more restless. It was too nice a morning to drive himself crazy thinking about it, he decided. He gazed out toward the ocean to see if anyone was in trouble. Finding no one in any immediate danger, he took off his T-shirt and high-tops and leaned back in his chair to take in some rays. The warm sun beating down on him made his first hour on duty more tolerable.

Some time after noon, while Fury scanned the water yet again for weak swimmers, he spotted his surfing buddies, Nick and Danny, up on the decks of their boards. With their punky haircuts and board shorts with wild patterns, Fury would recognize them anywhere. Nick's bright pink, yellow, and aqua wide-striped shorts would look radical with his new pink high-tops and his new hair, Fury thought. Maybe he could talk him into swapping them for a couple of T-shirts he had that Nick liked.

Fury envied Nick and Danny's freedom so much! He watched his friends paddle out beyond the swell, snag a wave, and ride the glassy smooth surf in again. That was what he had planned to do all summer; if only he could join them! But he knew that was out of the question, at least while he was relieving Leslie. Fury watched Nick and Danny as they beached their boards on the next ride in. They spotted Fury on the tower and waved to him. As he waved back to them, he had an idea how to relieve his boredom. There would be nothing wrong with going over and just talking to them for a few minutes. After all, he could keep an eye out for trouble at the water's edge as well as he could from the tower. Jeff would have no reason to get on his case—he was only stretching his legs so that he'd be ready for any emergencies. Jumping down the last few steps, Fury left the tower and headed for the shore. The sand was hot and he hopped from one foot to the other as he walked across it.

"Want to try out my hot new board?" Nick called out to Fury as he ran toward the water.

Excited, Fury forgot about everything else, even the fact that the sand had practically singed the bottoms of his feet.

"When did you get it?" he asked Nick.

"The day before yesterday."

"Are you sure I can try it?"

"Sure I'm sure. Just as long as you don't ding it."

"You're on!" Fury snatched off his shades, yanked his Walkman out of his back pocket, his earphones from around his neck and handed everything to Danny.

"Hold this stuff for me," he said, then jumped

on the board and paddled out to catch a wave. Even before he was up on the light, fiberglass board, he could tell it was built to shred. Playing it loose and fast, he stood up and dropped in on a wave; he could feel that he had a good board beneath him. He rode the swell into shore, then beached Nick's new board.

"Man, it's radical. I've got to get back to the chair now. But thanks for the ride, Nick. You're one lucky dude."

"And you're one unlucky dude, Fury. Here comes Jeff," Danny announced as he handed Fury his belongings.

Fury handed Nick his board, then slipped his shades back on and tried to act cool, like Jeff hadn't caught him doing anything wrong. "How's it going, Jeff? Need me anywhere else today?" he asked, acting as if standing around with Nick and Danny was all part of the job.

"Didn't Leslie relay my message to you?" Jeff inquired. He didn't bother to respond to Fury's question, nor did he greet Nick or Danny. He glared directly at Fury.

"What message?" Fury had a pretty good idea what Jeff was getting at, but he wanted to hear it straight from Jeff. Maybe Jeff wouldn't have the guts to say it to his face.

"I told her to tell you that I've had it with your lateness. If you want to know the truth, I've just about had it with you."

"Oh, that message." Fury said out of the side

of his mouth. He didn't tell Jeff that the feeling was mutual.

"I also told her to tell you that if you were out of line once more, I'd have no choice but to fire you. And it looks as if you were way out of line just now, unless you can explain what you were doing on a surfboard while you're supposed to be on duty. Practicing rescue techniques?"

"Hey, cool it, Jeff," Nick began. "It really wasn't Fury's fault. He wasn't doing anything wrong—"

"Thanks, Nick, but don't waste your breath," Fury cut in. He had reached the point where he'd just as soon not bother to explain anything to Jeff, especially when he was being so condescending to him. "Jeff's had it with me, and I've had it with this job. I was thinking about quitting anyway. So now's as good a time as any. I'll save you the trouble of firing me, Jeff. I quit!"

Fury felt better the second he told Jeff he was through with lifeguarding. What he needed was a change of scene—more surfing and less sitting around. But his sense of relief was quickly followed by a wave of guilt for having abandoned his post before Leslie got back. "As of tomorrow, you can start looking for a new relief man," he added, feeling the need to finish the day for Leslie's sake.

"As of now, you mean. I'll cover for you the rest of the day," Jeff said.

"Okay, by me. Why slave the day away when I could be doing something fun like surfing with

Nick and Danny?" Fury noticed that his friend
was wearing a waterproof Casio. "What time do
you have?" he asked Danny.

"Five to one."

"Great! The day's still young. I'm picking up
my skateboard and shoes, then I'm heading
home to get my board. I'll meet you guys back
here at two," Fury told his friends, deliberately
ignoring Jeff. As far as Fury was concerned, the
senior lifeguard didn't exist.

But a minute later as he collected his stuff at
his lifeguard station, he almost felt like thanking
Jeff for forcing him to quit before the senior
lifeguard had a chance to fire him. Now he was
as free as a bird. He could spend his summer the
way he had always intended to—surfing from
sunup to sundown—from as far north as Rincon
to as far south as Laguna Beach. "The summer
has now officially begun!" Fury sang out as he
hurried across the sand to Surfrider.

Chapter 4

Fury stepped off the hot sand onto the sidewalk, set his skateboard beside him, and sat down on the curb to put on his high-tops. As he yanked on a sneaker he chuckled to himself. The day was getting better and better.

"Where are you off to?"

Fury looked up from putting on his other high-top and saw Leslie, hands on hips, standing in front of him.

"So, where are you off to?" She sounded even more annoyed the second time she said it. "I'm not even back from lunch yet."

"Jeff's no longer on the verge of firing me. I quit as of five minutes ago."

"Who's on my tower?" A worry line came across Leslie's face. Fury thought it looked really out of character. To him, Leslie, with her long blond hair bleached even lighter by the sun, her all-over copper tan, and in her red Speedo and red shorts, almost always looked as if she had just stepped out of a suntan lotion ad.

Fury didn't like seeing normally happy-go-lucky Leslie frowning, and quickly added, "Don't worry. Jeff's covering for me."

"What about tomorrow?" she asked.

"I'm sure he'll find a replacement for me by then," Fury said.

"What if he doesn't?"

Leslie's barrage of questions was making Fury feel frustrated. He couldn't seem to say anything to make her happy, and he was getting tired of trying. "It's not up to me to find one, Leslie. Look, I've gotta go. I'm meeting some people in an hour."

"Rough life. Thanks a lot, Fury. It's nice to know I can depend on you," Leslie said, the worried expression on her face quickly changing to one of annoyance.

By now Fury couldn't care less whether she was ticked off with him again or not. The whole world was, so why should Leslie be an exception? What mattered most to him now was making tracks to the house to pick up his surfboard and getting back to the beach again.

Unfortunately, Russ had other ideas. "What do you plan to do about the towels?" he demanded the minute Fury walked into the house.

Fury couldn't help answering Russ's question with a couple of his own. "Hey, Russ, what did *you* do today? Stay home just waiting for me to walk through the door so you could ask me that question?" The way people were on his case today, he didn't doubt it.

"You wish. I wouldn't waste my day waiting for you to show up *anywhere*. Not that it's any of your business, I'm waiting for a phone call from this mechanic named Mike. He might have a job for me in his auto-repair shop. If some people around here paid their rent on time, I wouldn't need to look for a job. But I don't want to get into that now."

Fury was glad he didn't. He had heard Russ's comments about paying his rent on time too many times before. And he wasn't in the mood to think about how he would pay this month's rent now that he had quit his job.

"Let's get back to the towels. What do you plan to do with them?" Russ asked again.

Fury was happy that Russ had changed the subject for him. "What do you *want* me to do with them? Put them away? I don't have a problem with that. But I just walked in. So, chill out, Russ. I'll get to it in a minute." Fury was getting pretty tired of Russ pouncing on him every time he turned around.

But Fury found out soon enough that Russ had a good reason to be mad, for once. Flinging open the accordian-style door to the utility closet, and then the door to the dryer, Russ yanked out three red-spotted towels and waved them in front of Fury's face. "How am I going to explain this to my parents when they get back from their vacation in Europe? I thought you said the dye washes out. Washes *in* would be more like it."

"I'm sorry, man. I thought it would come out. Maybe it will if I run the towels through the washer again."

"Be my guest." Russ tossed the towels to Fury. "I'll be outside waiting for the results. If the phone rings, I'll answer it." Fury figured from the way Russ was dressed in just his bright yellow jams that besides waiting for his call, he'd been spending the afternoon sunbathing on the deck. Well, at least one of them was having a good day.

Fury threw the towels and an extra cap of liquid laundry detergent back into the washing machine and turned it on. He'd have to wait for the washing cycle to be completed, about fifteen minutes, before he could put them in the dryer. The three heavy bath towels would probably take about forty-five minutes to dry. It would be at least an hour, he calculated, before he could get out of the house again. So much for his plan to meet Nick and Danny at two o'clock.

He plodded into the den and plopped into a beanbag chair near the freestanding fireplace. Why was he feeling so tired? he wondered. It was only the beginning of the afternoon. He must have gotten up too early this morning, and that was why nothing had gone right for him all day. Perhaps he should just get back into bed, pull the covers over his head, and go to sleep. As good as the idea sounded to him, he'd only have to get up in another ten minutes to throw the towels into the dryer. Fury heard the phone ring in the kitchen. Following Russ's instructions, he sank deeper into the beanbag chair and made no effort to get up and answer it.

"Hey, Fury, it's for you!" Russ shouted from the kitchen.

Of course it was for him, he groaned, now that he had made himself so comfortable that it was almost impossible to get up out of the chair. It was probably Tracy wanting to apologize or wondering why he hadn't called or stopped in to see her. He thought about whether he was ready to forgive her for hurting his feelings. Considering how badly everyone else had treated him that day, Tracy had actually been nice to him in comparison. He tried standing up, but he couldn't lift himself so he turned on his side and rolled out of the stuffed, brown vinyl chair onto the carpet. As he sat up, he saw Russ standing in the doorway to the den holding the portable phone.

"Oh, how cute. You roll over and sit up. Do you do any other tricks?"

Fury felt a smile coming on but stifled it. He wasn't about to laugh at any of Russ's jokes. "Thanks," he said matter-of-factly as Russ handed him the phone and left the den.

"Fury, it's me, Danny," his friend said on the other end.

Although he was glad that Danny had called, Fury couldn't help feeling a little disappointed that Tracy hadn't.

"I'm glad I caught you,"Danny went on. "Turns out we won't be able to meet you as planned. Nick wiped out and smashed his head on his board."

Not wanting Russ to overhear his conversation, Fury waited until he heard the sliding glass door to the deck slam shut. Then he said to Danny, "That's a shame about Nick. How badly was he hurt? Is he all right now?"

"He's not feeling all that terrific. Dizzy, mostly. We're going to call it a day."

"Good idea. Man, what a tough break," Fury said.

"Yeah. Look, maybe we can hang out tomorrow. I think Nick will recover by then. He always bounces right back."

"Okay. Why don't we meet at the Surfrider Cafe for breakfast, like at eleven? Tell Nick I hope his hard head didn't damage his new board. Just kidding. Tell him I hope he feels better. Thanks for calling."

"No problem. See you tomorrow," Danny said just before hanging up.

Fury walked into the kitchen and hung up the portable phone. It was too bad that Nick had injured himself, but at least now Fury wouldn't be a no-show and tick his buddies off. He checked the digital clock on the microwave and saw that he had another five minutes to kill before the load of laundry would be done—which was just enough time to make himself something to eat.

He opened the fridge, helped himself to a package of lunch meat, some cheese, and a half of a loaf of French Bread. He wolfed down a hero sandwich and was about to clean up when he heard the washing machine shut off. Leaving the remaining meat and cheese and a couple of knives out on the kitchen counter, he scurried into the hallway and took the towels out of the washing machine.

"Way to go," he whooped as he raced out of the house and onto the deck to show Russ the results. "Hey, Russ, check these out!" he hollered, spreading the towels out on the deck. "The stains came out."

"Oh, these towels look like new again! I never thought those nasty stains would come out. What brand laundry detergent did you use? I've just got to get to the store and buy some," Russ quipped in a high-pitched voice.

This time Fury couldn't stop himself from laughing even if he tried. Besides finding Russ's imitation of a woman doing a soap commercial really funny, he found himself laughing extra hard out of sheer relief. His laughter was infectious, and Russ soon joined in. When their laughing jag was over, Fury could tell that Russ was as relieved as he was that the dye had washed out. And, best of all, Russ didn't appear to be upset with Fury anymore.

Of course, Fury knew he could change Russ's mood in a minute. When Russ had asked him last week for next month's rent, Fury had headed him off by telling him he'd give it to him when he got his next paycheck. Now all Fury had to tell him was that he had quit his job and there wouldn't be much of a next paycheck. Fury decided to bring up Russ's favorite subject instead. "Been playing any volleyball lately?" Now that Fury had some free time, he wouldn't mind getting in a few games himself.

"Whenever I can. Why don't you join us? You know where to find me, don't you?"

"Sure. On volleyball court number two." Everyone, including Fury, knew that Russ and his friend Chris dominated the volleyball games on Marina Bay Beach. Two-man teams came from miles around to try to beat them, but never succeeded. Fury thought it would be fun sometime to see how he and a partner could do against Russ and Chris. But now, looking down at the towels on the deck, he said, "I'd better go throw these into the dryer." As long as he and Russ were on friendly terms again, Fury figured he'd better quit while he was ahead.

Now that the towel crisis was over and he didn't have to worry about Russ being angry, Fury decided that he could really use a nap. He tossed the towels in the dryer and headed for the den. After removing his high-tops, he stretched out on the daybed. But instead of nodding right off as he thought he would, he started reviewing all the ups and downs of the day. Basically, it had been divided into two parts: the down part, where he had upset Leslie, Russ, Tracy, and Jeff, all in a few hours: then the up part, this afternoon, quitting and getting the hair dye out of the towels. Somehow those two didn't balance out.

As long as he couldn't fall right to sleep, he decided to update who was and who wasn't still mad at him. Talking to him at the moment were Nick, Danny, Jed, and now Russ, although he didn't know for how long.

Leslie, Jeff, and Tracy were still mad at him. Fury knew that Jeff was a lost cause. And he'd never had much luck bringing Leslie around to his point of view, either. She could hold a grudge longer than anybody he'd ever met. However, he and Tracy could never stay mad at each other for long. . . .

He was sure that by the end of the night they'd be talking to each other again. Even if Tracy didn't apologize to him first, Fury decided that he would. Just because she didn't like his hair he couldn't stay mad at the love of his life. In a few days, maybe he'd even thoroughly rinse out the pink part and redye it platinum just to show her how much he cared about her. He closed his eyes and thought about how they'd kiss and make up later. Somehow their attraction for each other was always stronger after they'd had

an argument—maybe that was why they fought
as much as they did, Fury mused. He imagined
himself gently covering Tracy's neck with little
kisses, stroking her wild, jet-black hair, then
nuzzling his face in it. After all that had gone
wrong for him today, he needed a shoulder to
cry on. Thinking that there wasn't a softer one
than Tracy's, he finally dozed off.

Chapter 5

Fury was only dozing when he heard the front door. Two telephone calls had disturbed his sleep earlier. He had been sleeping with one ear open ever since, more or less waiting for Tracy to come home; he hoped she just had. He thought he heard the sound of her cowboy boots clopping across the hardwood entryway, so he got out of bed.

Next he heard the refrigerator door slam shut, then the sound of boots clumping upstairs. He was sure now that Tracy was home. What he wasn't sure about was how long he had slept or exactly what time it was now, but he figured it must be sometime after five o'clock. Tracy usually got home around then, grabbed a cold drink from the fridge, and ran upstairs to change into her bathing suit. She always spent the hours right after work on the back deck, catching the last warm rays of the day and relaxing for a while. Fury always looked forward to seeing her when she came home from work and even though they had fought this morning, this afternoon was no exception.

In fact, this was his favorite time of day. The sun was still quite bright overhead, but the air temperature was a little cooler than at midafternoon. He and Tracy had a standing date out on the back deck for around five-thirty. This was their special time together to unwind from work and to catch up on the news of the day.

Tonight especially, Fury had plenty to share with Tracy. But before he got around to telling her all that had happened to him today, he had made up his mind to apologize to Tracy before she got a chance to apologize to him. He had made enough enemies in one day, and he didn't want to count the one person who really cared about him among them.

Fury took the fact that Tracy hadn't broken their routine as a good sign. *She's probably as eager as I am to make up. If she isn't, why would she bother to keep our late-afternoon date on the deck?* Fury thought as he threw off his red lifeguard shorts, more than glad to be out of them for good, and threw on a pair of more normal-looking, blue-and-white-striped jams. But as he rushed out of the den to join Tracy, he had second thoughts about appearing to be so eager. He went back into his room, picked up his Walkman, and slipped on his shades and his earphones. Just in case Tracy wasn't quite ready to greet him with open arms, he decided to play down his entrance.

He stepped out on the deck and saw Tracy stretched out on the lounger with the portable phone beside her. Her head was buried in a copy of *Variety*, the daily newspaper of the entertainment trade. Leafing through it for possible gigs was apparently more important to her than making up with him, because she didn't even bother to look up. It appeared at first glance that Tracy was quite content to unwind from the day without him, and Fury was glad that he had decided to play it a little cool.

But his first impression was wrong. When she heard Fury close the sliding glass door behind him, Tracy looked up from her paper, then lovingly at him, as if she was really excited to see him. "Hey, honey," she said. "It's good to see you. I'm sorry I bummed you out this morning. I owe you—"

"Hold it, Tracy," he broke in. "That was going to be my opening line." A sheepish smirk came across Fury's face. It was never easy for him to apologize, but this time he was determined to beat Tracy to the punch. "I'm the one who should apologize to *you*. I don't know why I was being so sensitive."

"You had every right to be. I really jumped on you this morning about your hair," Tracy said.

"No, you didn't," Fury objected. "You were just playing around. I overreacted."

"No you didn't. I did."

"Maybe we both did, but I'm the one who should apologize first." There! He had done it! He had made his apology before Tracy did.

"I don't know why you should be the one to apologize first when I was the one who started the whole thing, who teased you about your hair," Tracy protested.

"Look, I've got a better idea. Instead of arguing about who should apologize to whom, let's just kiss and make up."

Fury could tell that Tracy liked that idea. She put down her paper and beckoned to Fury to sit down beside her on the lounger. Fury sat down on the edge and was about to kiss Tracy gently on the lips when the lounger, unable to support both their weights, collapsed underneath them.

The next thing Fury knew, his shades flew off him, his Walkman fell out of his hand, Tracy was sprawled on the deck, and he was on top of her. Fury was now very much aware that she was only wearing a bikini and what had started out as a sweet make-up kiss was now very definitely a passionate embrace. In the heat of the moment Tracy lifted her mouth to Fury's, and he could feel her love for him in her warm kiss. He kissed her back hard. He didn't need words to tell her how he felt about her, either. Kissing and making up in the flesh was turning out to be even better than Fury had imagined.

Suddenly the phone rang, and Tracy bolted upright, acting as if someone had walked in on them. Even though it was just the ringing of the phone that had interrupted them, she smoothed down her hair and straightened her swimsuit, in an attempt to gain her composure before picking up the phone.

"Hello? Oh, hi, Will," Tracy said, sounding a little breathless as she answered the phone.

"Now? Um, I can't. I'm in the middle of something." She turned to Fury and winked. "Okay, if it's that important, I'll come now. I'll see you in thirty minutes," she said with a look on her face that told Fury that she'd explain to him what was going on as soon as she got off the phone. As far as Fury was concerned, she really didn't have to bother. He had gotten the gist. Tracy was ditching him for Will—temporarily, at least.

When Tracy hung up and told him that Will was putting the program together for Nashville Night the following week and had to talk to her about her place in the lineup, Fury had already figured out as much. Although he was happy about Tracy's chance to advance her singing career, he wasn't particularly thrilled about Will's timing, or the fact that Tracy seemed so willing to run off and leave him.

"When will you be back? I was really looking forward to us spending some time together. I've got a lot to tell you," he said as Tracy began picking up her things.

"I know. Believe me, Fury, I'd rather stay home with you. But Will insisted on seeing me now. He has to bring the program to the printer tomorrow."

Fury understood Tracy's dilemma, but that didn't mean he liked the fact that she had to leave.

Tracy seemed to read his mind. "Listen, honey, I shouldn't be that long. Maybe an hour at the most. Why don't I meet you back here and we can talk over a late dinner? I hope I'll have lots to tell you, too. Then we can work on some of my numbers together. Why don't you warm up while I'm gone?" Tracy suggested. She leaned over and gave him a sweet kiss on the lips and added, "Before we get down to work, we can continue what Will so rudely interrupted out on the deck. But now I gotta go." Tracy threw him another kiss and flew upstairs, changed, and hurried out of the house.

Fury practically slunk back to his room, disappointed that his time with Tracy had been cut short by Will's phone call. Although he appreciated how much her meeting with Will meant to her, he also felt a little rejected. He picked up his bass, plugged it into his amplifier and, as Tracy had suggested, played several upbeat numbers to warm up. He felt better, but the time still passed slowly. He practiced some of the ballads they had worked on, but every song he played only reminded him that Tracy seemed to be gone much longer than she said she would be.

Why should I sit around and mope? Fury asked himself. *Tracy and Will probably finished their business a long time ago, and now they're out together having a good time. Otherwise, she'd be back by now,* Fury fumed. The more he thought about it, the angrier he got, until he couldn't sit in his room another second. What he needed, he decided, was some fresh air and company. He got up to see if anyone was around the house.

He found Russ and Leslie enjoying the sunset together on the deck. Russ greeted him with an angry glare.

"Fury, didn't I talk to you once today about cleaning up after yourself? It's bad enough that you raided the refrigerator this afternoon and ate Jed's food, but then, to add insult to injury, you left it out on the kitchen counter to spoil," he said.

This time Fury didn't even bother to make any excuses for himself. He hadn't known it was Jed's food he had eaten, but he knew when he was in the wrong. He also knew that he should have stayed cooped up in his room, at least until midnight. All he could do was wait for the day to end—tomorrow had to be better.

"I'm sorry, Russ," Fury apologized lamely. "I forgot. I guess I got distracted by the towels."

"Yeah. Well, now that we're on the subject, I suppose you forgot about them, too."

Fury slapped his forehead. He had fallen asleep and had completely forgotten to take the towels out of the dryer to put them away neatly as he had promised.

"I'll go do it now." Fury made a move to go back inside.

"Don't bother. I already did," Russ said.

"Then I'll go clean up the kitchen."

"Don't bother. I already did it," Leslie dittoed.

"Thanks," Fury muttered. Hearing how disappointed in him they both sounded, he could hardly get that one little word out.

"Why don't you sit down?" Russ asked in a pleasant-sounding voice.

Surprised by Russ's friendly offer, Fury sat down on a redwood bench. Maybe he could enjoy the rest of the warm evening with Russ and Leslie. But it looked as if round one was over, and round two was just beginning.

"Look, Fury," Russ began. "If it was just your flaky, irresponsible behavior I had to overlook, I could live with it. I'm used to it by now. But there's a limit to my understanding, patience, and most important, my money. I'm not renting rooms for free, you know. Maybe your parents or someone could wire you some money."

A hurt expression swept swiftly across Fury's face. Fury was sure that Russ knew that he didn't have any parents and that he'd grown up in foster homes. He had mentioned it to him a couple of weeks after he had moved in.

Russ looked embarrassed. "I'm sorry I said

that. I forgot about your family situation," he apologized. "But what I'm getting at is that your rent's more than two weeks overdue. You have to admit that I've waited long enough for you to pay up. And now Leslie just told me that you quit your job."

Fury looked with disappointment at Leslie, who lowered her eyes, unable to look him in the face. Without having to say a single word, her downcast eyes told Fury exactly how she felt. "I'm sorry, too," they told him. "I'm sorry I had to fink on you."

"Les and I have talked things over and we both agree that when Pamela gets back tomorrow morning, we need to hold a meeting to discuss some house problems. In the meantime, I want you to shape up."

Fury was surprised to learn that Pamela was coming back tomorrow. But he had a pretty good idea what, no, *whom* Russ meant by "house problems." It also didn't come as a great shock to him that by her silence Leslie was saying that she was in total agreement with Russ. He had no trouble re-creating the conversation that must have passed between brother and sister before he came out on the deck.

Now that he thought about it, how could he have been so naive as to think that they had simply been enjoying the sunset together? When Leslie came home, she must have told Russ about Fury's run-in with Jeff and how he had quit his job before Jeff got the chance to fire him. Then Russ must have suggested the meeting. And all he had to do to get Leslie to agree to it was remind her how she had goofed when she had originally rented the den to Fury without consulting him first. Leslie owed Russ one for that, and he obviously intended to collect from her now.

Not that she didn't have her own reasons to be upset with Fury. Jeff probably hadn't found a replacement for him yet, and Leslie, Fury figured, wasn't looking forward to a day on the lifeguard chair without any breaks.

So now he knew why Russ had so cordially invited him to sit down on the deck. It certainly wasn't to enjoy the full moon or the warm summer night with him and his sister. Fury decided he'd had enough of Russ Stevens for one day.

"I'm going for a walk on the beach. I don't know when I'll be back so don't bother to wait up for me," Fury exploded. He jumped up and off the redwood deck onto the sand and moved out, first in a fast-pace walk, then in an all-out sprint.

"Fury!" he heard Leslie call after him. "Don't do anything stupid."

Russ yelled something at him, too, but Fury raced down the beach until he was out of earshot. He couldn't get away from Russ fast enough. Catching his breath and his bearings, he looked toward the highway. By the light of the moon he could make out the outlines of the parcourse structures; he was about halfway to

Marina Bay, not far from the beach where he knew some surfers hung out at night. Until the neighbors complained to Russ about their broken beer bottles and rowdy behavior, they had hung out in front of the Stevenses' house. Sure enough, farther down the beach toward town, he spotted the surfers' bonfire.

Fury knew he wouldn't find Nick or Danny there; they didn't make a habit of hanging out with this crowd. When Fury first came down south from San Francisco, before Leslie had offered him a room to rent, he had crashed on the beach for a couple of nights. So he knew from experience that the Marina Bay surfers divided themselves into two groups: surfer bums, guys who didn't work, surfed all day, and went home at night; and the beach bums, the guys who didn't work, surfed all day, and slept on the beach at night. Nick and Danny were long-standing surfer bums, but they had parents to go home to and they steered clear of the beach bums. Fury knew that Nick and Danny thought these guys were a bunch of jerks, the way they ignored the Keep Marina Bay Clean signs and messed up the environment. Surfers who lived in town, as Nick and Danny did, hated it when the beach bums left trash on the sand, beer cans all over, and worst of all, broken beer bottles on the beach.

When things were going right for Fury, he could afford to share his surfing friends' opinion of the beach bums. But not tonight. Besides, he knew something about these guys that Nick and Danny would never have to know. If you were lonely, or desperate, and needed a place to crash, they'd never turn a stranger away from their campfire.

"Hey, Fury, is that you? Sit down and have a beer with me and tell me where you've been," someone called out to him when Fury stepped into the light of the blazing fire.

Fury looked at all the glowing faces around the campfire. Only one of them looked familiar, but that didn't surprise him. The beach bums moved up and down the coast, from one beach to another. The guy he recognized had been nicknamed Goofy because he surfed goofyfoot, with his left foot instead of his right foot forward on the board. There was one other thing about Goofy that everyone knew: He could fly into a rage if you said the wrong thing or looked at him the wrong way. However, he'd always been friendly enough toward Fury, and tonight seemed to be no exception. Looking at Goofy again, Fury remembered why he had thought the nickname suited him so well—he had two big front teeth that made him look like the famous cartoon character.

"Hey, man, what's wrong? You look like you just lost your best friend," Goofy said as Fury settled down next to him in the sand.

"Nothing's wrong. Where's that beer you were talking about?" Fury asked, figuring that the sooner he drank it, the quicker he could forget about Russ and all his other troubles.

"Right here." Goofy lifted a Corona out of the six-pack in the sand beside him and removed the cap with his teeth. Grinning, he handed the bottle to Fury. "Cheers," he said, clinking his bottle with Fury's. "And cheer up, man."

"Cheers," Fury said. He picked up the beer and drank the entire thing in one gulp. Putting down the bottle beside him, he wiped his mouth with the corner of his T-shirt. "There. That's much better." Russ's harsh words and the rest of his horrible day were already becoming a vague memory.

"Mighty big thirst you had there," Goofy commented. "I'll offer you another one, but this time you have to promise to be a little more sociable and fill me in on what you've been doing." Goofy opened a second bottle with his teeth and passed it over to Fury.

"Oh, yeah. I'm sorry."

Fury nursed this one, sipping it slowly, but he still didn't feel like talking.

"So, man, c'mon," Goofy prompted him. "Tell me, what have you been up to? I haven't seen you surfing, and you haven't been hanging out here, so you must be up to something else. Now I know I've got that right."

Fury sighed. The second beer, even more than Goofy's friendliness, loosened Fury up and made him want to pour out his troubles. "Well, if you want to know the truth, you were close when you said I looked like I lost my best friend. My girl friend went out earlier tonight to meet this guy about some gig and she still hasn't come back."

"Hey, relax, man. By the time we finish this six-pack, she'll be back. But by then, maybe you won't want to go home."

"Yeah. You're probably right," Fury said, then chugged the rest of his beer. After he set down the second empty next to the first one, he began to feel a lot better. So what if Tracy stayed out with Will? What did he care? *It's not like we're married,* Fury said to himself.

"So, where have you been hiding yourself these days?"

"Well, I was working for a while, but that's history. As of today I'm a free man. So you'll be seeing a lot more of me on the water. What about you? Still surfing backward?" Fury asked.

"Hey, watch what you say, man, or you'll find your head's screwed on backward," Goofy said roughly.

Fury got nervous for a moment. He had obviously said the wrong thing, and Goofy looked as if he wanted to kill him. But when Goofy threw back his head and started to laugh, Fury knew he had only been putting him on. Fury laughed along with him.

After that, everything they said, whether it was funny or not, made them laugh until their sides hurt. When they knocked off the last of the beers, the only thing they took seriously was the problem of finding another six-pack.

"I'd made a trip to the store, but in this hick town everything's sealed up tight as a drum this time of night," Goofy complained.

"Why don't I sneak back into the house and get a few cans out of the fridge?" Fury suggested, having completely forgotten his problems with Tracy, Russ, and everyone in the house.

"Hey, man, that's brilliant. I'll wait for you here. Save our spot, you know. When you get back, we can kick back, drink some more beer, and you can tell me the rest of your troubles. I've got all night."

Fury got to his feet. He'd do anything for a buddy like Goofy. This guy was a *real* friend—not like two-faced Russ, or Tracy, or Leslie.

"If I run, it shouldn't take me that long," Fury said as he took off. But after he ran a few yards down the beach, he began to wonder if he would make it back to the Stevens house at all.

Slowing to a walk, Fury concentrated on making a straight line to the beach house. If felt as if his legs weighed a ton, and he had to keep blinking to make sure he was still awake.

Fury slowly staggered the last few steps to the house and sat down on the edge of the deck, attempting to steady himself. Although he didn't feel all that terrific at the moment, he did think that getting bombed with Goofy had been one of his better ideas. The beers had done what he couldn't do without them, blotted everyone out of his brain, along with everything awful that had happened to him that day. And in fact, by the time the beers had taken their full effect, it had been after midnight. In that case, Fury now corrected himself, *yesterday* had been a big mistake. And he intended to keep it that way.

Just as soon as he felt steady enough to stand up, he'd creep into the house and make off with some more beer. He got up, still feeling shaky, and noticed that all the lights in the house were out. Good. If everyone was asleep, he wouldn't have to worry about waking anyone up, or tiptoeing around. He could just walk right into the kitchen and help himself to the beer—if he could walk. At the moment, just standing up made him feel woozy and he has to sit down again. He stretched out on the deck to try and stop his head from spinning, and the balmy night air covered him like a blanket.

Chapter 6

The next thing Fury felt was the early-morning sun shining on him. He opened his eyes and looked around. *What am I doing out on the deck*? He wondered. He remembered it had been pretty warm out the night before but that still didn't explain why he had decided to sleep under the stars. He tried to re-create the events of the previous evening, though he had such a bad headache that he could barely think straight. In spite of the pain, he began to piece things together. When he finally figured out how he had ended up sleeping outside, Fury felt much less disoriented, but his head still felt awful. He needed a cup of strong coffee—fast.

To his surprise he found Tracy in the kitchen, and she had already made a pot of coffee.

"Fury, your hair's a mess!" she cried. "You look awful. Where have you been all night? I was worried sick about you," she remarked.

"Good morning to you, too. If you can't say anything nice about my hair, would you do me a favor and just shut up about it?" Fury said crossly.

"Don't be so sensitive. I only said that it looked a little messy," Tracy said.

"Well, I am sensitive. So leave me alone." Fury instinctively started tugging at his hair in a vain attempt to give his slept-on spikes some life. Then he tucked his wrinkled T-shirt into his even more crumpled shorts.

"Okay, okay. Let's not argue about your hair again. It looks marvelous, simply marvelous. Now where were you last night?" Tracy asked again.

"Where were *you* all night?" Fury countered. "I thought you were just going into town to talk to Will about the program and you'd be back in an *hour*. But you went out with that sleaze afterward, didn't you?" Fury retaliated. He walked over to the electric coffee maker, took a mug off the cup rack next to it, and poured himself a cupful. He sipped it while he waited anxiously for Tracy to answer him. The coffee did little for his headache, but at least it woke him up.

Tracy stared at Fury. "First of all, I don't know why I'm even bothering to account for my evening after that nasty remark you made about

Will. You have no right to call him a sleaze. And second of all, I did not go out with him. I went out with Jed."

"Jed?" Fury couldn't believe his ears. He certainly couldn't be jealous of Jed. Tracy hardly ever spoke more than two words to Jed, let alone spent any time with him. But that only made Fury more curious to know why Tracy had gone out with him. "How did you end up going out with Jed?"

"Simple. I went into town and met with Will for a little while. Our *business* meeting took a little longer than I had expected, for which I am truly sorry. But as it so happens, Will wants me to headline Nashville Night. That's what took so long. I had to go over the list of numbers I'll be doing with him," Tracy explained. "Anyway, when I did come home you had already gone out. I asked Leslie if she knew where you were. She told me you and Russ had had a big argument and you had split. Since I hadn't had any dinner, Jed invited me to go get a bite to eat with him. That's it. That's what I did last night." Tracy paused. "Now it's your turn."

Fury was still thirsty, and he walked over to the refrigerator to get out some milk. He immediately noticed the memo in Russ's handwriting posted on the door: IMPORTANT MEETING—7:30 P.M.—FRIDAY NIGHT—EVERYONE PLEASE BE THERE TO DISCUSS HOUSE PROBLEMS—THANKS. Fury shook his head. Taking the carton of milk out, he headed into the dining room with his empty coffee cup in the other hand. Tracy, followed him in and sat down next to him at the dining room table.

Fury wished his explanation for the previous night's events was as clear and uncomplicated as Tracy's. He didn't really know where to start, but the memo, he decided, was as good as place as any. "Did you see the note Russ posted on the refrigerator?" he asked Tracy.

"I saw it last night when I came home. Russ was already upstairs so I didn't get a chance to ask him what it was about. Do you know?" Tracy inquired.

"No. But I have my suspicions. I think I'm the 'house problem.' I also think Russ wants me to move out," Fury told her.

"Fury, he can't do that! Why? What happened?" Tracy asked, sounding concerned.

Fury poured himself a glass of milk, gulped it down, then poured out the whole story; how he had gotten upset when Tracy hadn't come home, how he had gone out on the deck to talk with Russ and Leslie, and how Russ had gotten on his case again about not paying the rent on time.

"Why didn't you just tell him that you'd give him the money as soon as you got paid?" Tracy said.

"I wish I could. But I quit my lifeguard job yesterday. That's what I wanted to talk to you about when you came home from work."

"Oh, Fury," Tracy sighed. "No wonder you're so annoyed at me for going off to meet Will. If I had only known, I swear, I would have put off my meeting with Will until tomorrow. But don't worry about it—we'll figure something out. I'll help you look for another job." She reached across the table and patted Fury on the arm.

"Tracy, I'm not interested in another job just now," Fury said.

"Of course you are! But we'll talk more about that later. Get on with what happened last night."

"Well, after my argument with Russ, I felt like I was about to explode. I jumped off the deck, angry at Russ, Jeff, you, the whole world! I raced across the beach until I reached a campfire, and this guy I know invited me to have a beer with him. He was real friendly and offered me another one, and one more after that. I staggered home so drunk that I couldn't even make it into the house." Fury decided to leave out his reason for returning to the house. "I crashed on the deck. That's all. I slept out there last night."

"Oh, Fury, I'm so sorry I wasn't there when you needed me. If only Will hadn't called," Tracy apologized, getting up from her chair. She wrapped her arms around him and gave him a bear hug.

Fury squeezed Tracy tightly to him and started stroking her hair. "I'm sorry I called Will a sleaze. Congratulations on getting top billing. I always knew you'd be going places," Fury said, feeling happy for Tracy, but a little sad for himself. Just when her career was beginning to take off, he seemed to be bottoming out. But he didn't want to think about that now, not when he had Tracy so close to him. He held her head in his hands and kissed her sweetly, more out of appreciation for her support than out of passion.

Suddenly Tracy pulled away from him. "Talking about going places, I'm scheduled to open the store this morning. Why don't we meet for lunch so we can talk more?"

"I'd love to, but I've already made plans to have breakfast and then go surfing with Nick and Danny," Fury said.

"Don't you think you ought to look for another job?"

"Tracy, don't lay a guilt trip on me. Let's get something straight right now. I came down to Marina Bay to surf and that's what I intend to do until I'm good and ready to look for a job. So let's drop the subject."

"I didn't mean to pressure you." Tracy said, smoothing Fury's T-shirt with her fingers. "It's just that I care what happens to you. I don't want Russ to have any reason to kick you out of the house. But if you want me to drop the subject, the subject's dropped. How about getting together before the house meeting?"

"You're on!" Fury agreed.

"Let's plan your strategy over dinner. Why don't you meet me at the store at five-thirty?" Tracy asked, starting to lift herself off Fury's lap.

"Wait a sec. Not so fast," Fury protested. "I

like that perfume you're wearing. You don't usually wear it to work, do you?" Fury put his arms around Tracy's waist and pulled her back down onto his lap.

But before Fury could kiss her, Tracy pulled away from him again. "I'm really running late," she said, standing up to go. "Sorry, hon. I'll see you tonight."

As Tracy was leaving the dining room, Fury noticed that in her white satin cowgirl blouse, black leather pants, and white boots, she was more dressed up than usual for work. But he had a hunch that Tracy had preplanned their reconciliation and had gotten all dolled up for *him*. He knew she couldn't stay mad at him for more than a day. Well, the truth was that he couldn't stay mad at her, either. He made a mental note to look extra good for his date with Tracy that night. It also occurred to him that it wouldn't hurt his cause to look decent for the house meeting.

It also wouldn't hurt, he decided, if he turned over a new leaf and started cleaning up after himself. He walked back into the kitchen carrying both his and Tracy's coffee mugs, washed them out, and hung them up on the cup rack. As he was putting the milk away, he checked the time on the microwave. It blinked nine-forty-five. No wonder Tracy was in such a hurry. Now that he knew how late it was, he needed to get moving, too.

He jumped out of his sandy clothes and into a

cold shower. It did the trick; it got rid of his gritty feeling and his hangover. He stepped out of the shower a new man. Today, he thought, unlike yesterday, had gotten off to a really great start. And with plans to go surfing with Nick and Danny, then to have dinner with Tracy, it could only get better. Before rushing out of the house, he made a point of straightening up the bathroom after he was done using it.

Fury picked out a couple of Nick's favorite T-shirts to use in a trade. He purposely wore Tracy's favorite T-shirt, a dinosaur on a surfboard with the words Original Surf Monster, underneath it, and a pair of bright green board shorts. Then he put on fake emerald earrings to tie the whole outfit together. Tracy liked the way Fury looked in green. Too bad, he now thought, as he admired himself in the mirror, he hadn't gone for the green dye job yesterday. Oh, well, he mused, he could always dye it green when he got tired of the pink. In the meantime he could trade his T-shirts for Nick's pink, yellow, and aqua–striped shorts—and with his pink hair and pink high-tops, he could still put together a pretty raw look. He laced up his high-tops, slipped on his shades, and put his wallet in his back pocket. Grabbing his long surfing board from his closet, he collected the shirts for Nick from off his bed and headed out the door.

As soon as Fury stepped outside into the sunshine, he felt like a man who had just been released from prison. There was no way he was going to spend another summer day feeling pent up, sitting in that lifeguard chair, being a spectator, and watching everybody else around him having fun in the sun. So what if Tracy thought he should get another job. The only thing Fury cared about right now was catching his first ride in on a wave.

It was exactly eleven o'clock when Fury strode into the Surfrider Cafe to meet Nick and Danny for breakfast. They were about to sit down at a table by the window at the front of the cafe—which had a great view of the beach. Fury walked up to the table, leaned his surfboard against a wall, and sat down with them.

"Hey, dude, little early for St. Patrick's Day, but I still like your outfit," Nick teased him.

Nick isn't much for words, Fury thought as a grin spread across his face, *but when he does say something it's usually pretty funny.*

"I've brought you something that might improve yours," Fury shot back, holding up two of his T-shirts that Nick had admired: one was aqua with the ocean Pacific logo on it, and the other was a bright yellow T-shirt with the saying Surf Till It Hurts printed in red on it. "I guess you took the saying on this shirt a little too seriously yesterday," Fury said, pointing to the words. "How are you feeling today?"

"Much better. Luckily, I'm still in one piece. More important, so is my board," Nick said, smiling.

"I'm glad. Now, on to more pressing matters. Want to trade these shirts for the board shorts you had on yesterday?"

"You've got a deal. I'll give them to you tomorrow," Nick said.

"I don't know about you two guys, but I came here to eat breakfast, not to attend a clothing swap. I'm going up to the counter to order," Danny informed his friends, getting up from the table.

"We're coming," Fury said, putting the T-shirts down on the table.

As Fury trailed over to the counter after Danny, he thought he saw Tracy sitting at a table in the rear under a hanging fern with Will, the owner of the cafe. Will had his arm around the back of Tracy's chair—no, on closer look, Fury could see that it was around her *shoulder. It couldn't be Tracy*, Fury said to himself, but he knew better. He'd recognized that full head of jet-black hair anywhere, not to mention the white satin blouse, black leather pants, and white boots he had seen her in a little over an hour ago.

How could he have been so stupid as to believe she had put on that outfit for *his* benefit? Fury asked himself as he banged his head with his fist. It killed him even more to think that Will was breathing in her sensuous perfume at this very moment. No wonder she was wearing it this morning!

"What can I get you?" the counterman asked Fury after Danny ordered some eggs.

Fury just stood there, unable to answer.

"What'll it be?" the counterman asked again.

"Oh, nothing. I'm not hungry," Fury finally muttered, backing away from the counter.

"What's with you?" Nick asked him.

"I don't know. I lost my appetite."

"You don't look so good. Are you sick or something?" Nick asked.

"Yeah. I'm sick. Sick and disgusted. Look over there." Fury turned his head in Tracy's direction just in time to see her give Will a kiss on his cheek.

"It looks like you lost more than your appetite," Nick remarked.

"C'mon, Nick. Cut the comedy."

"I'm sorry, Fury. Do you want to take off?" Nick asked in a more understanding voice.

"I think I'd better. If I stick around and see any more, I might do something I'd regret. Danny, we're leaving!"

"What about my eggs?" Danny asked, still waiting for his order.

"Let him eat his breakfast. Without it, he's impossible. Then we'll leave," Nick said to Fury.

"All right. I'll wait for you guys at the table. I'm not hungry," Fury said, reluctantly giving in to Nick's request.

Nick stepped up to the counter to order his breakfast while Fury headed back to their table. But his better judgment told him that he really should leave before he got any angrier. He picked up his board, deciding to wait for his friends outside. But in spite of his attempt to keep his emotions in check, and leave before he got into trouble, Fury found himself sauntering up to Tracy and Will's table instead of out the door.

"Well, good morning," he greeted them. "If it isn't the singing sensation from Fresno, Tracy Berberian! What a surprise to see you here. May I have your autograph? Unless, of course, you're too busy," Fury said in a sarcastic tone.

Tracy looked up, obviously surprised to see Fury standing there. From the shocked expression on her face, he could tell that she was equally bewildered by his rude comments.

"Hello, Fury. You know Will, don't you?" Tracy said, apparently not knowing what else she should say.

"Of course I know Will. Everybody in town knows Will. His reputation for stealing other guys' girls is widespread. And now I know why you had to run off this morning—you're obviously in the middle of another one of those important *business* meetings. Right, Tracy?"

"For your information, yes, I am. I stopped in to get a cup of coffee, and Will asked me to sit down with him so he could show me the layout for the program before it went off to the printer," Tracy explained.

Fury watched Will's face turn the same shade of red as his neat little beard. "I hope this jerk isn't a friend of yours, Tracy," he said angrily. "Because I'm not going to sit here and let him insult me in my own cafe. I'm going to throw him right out of here."

Will got up from his captain's chair and walked over to Fury. He looked down at him menacingly from his six-foot-five height.

"Just try laying a hand on me," Fury said boldly. "If you touch me, I'll walk right out of here, up the street, and into the police station," Fury threatened.

Will backed off. "So, he's a troublemaker, too. You'd better get your friend out of here fast, Tracy, because the way I'm feeling toward him right now, I don't care *who* he tells." Then, turning to Tracy, in a softer voice, "You know, I don't think it's such a good idea for you to headline the show after all."

Tracy turned toward Fury, her eyes filling with tears.

"Thanks a lot for ruining my one big chance," she said. "In other words, everything." A single tear ran down Tracy's cheek as she stared at Fury. "You're not my friend. Why don't you get out of here?"

"Tracy, I'm sorry. I didn't mean to upset you like this. It's just that I got so mad seeing you with Will," Fury tried to explain.

"Get lost, pal," Will ordered.

Knowing he had seriously blown it, Fury turned away from Tracy without saying another word, swooped up his board, and stormed out of the cafe. Then he cut across Surfrider without looking and raced aimlessly across the sand. Nick and Danny, their short boards tucked under their arms, chased after him until they caught up with him at the water's edge.

"Hey, man, look. Surf's up. Want to try my new board again?" Nick asked, trying to catch his breath.

"Sure," Fury answered, distracted by the cozy image of Will and Tracy together in his head.

Look at that perfect wave out there," Nick said, still trying to lift Fury's spirits.

"Yeah. Listen, guys, thanks for trying, but I'm just not for surfing anymore. I'd only scrub and hurt myself like Nick did," Fury said, shrugging. "I think I'll cut out and just go home."

"What do you say we shred some waves?" Danny asked Nick.

"But what are you going to do, Fury?" Nick asked him.

"I think I'll just sit here for a while. Then I'll head home. You guys go on without me."

"You sure?" Nick asked, sounding concerned.

"I'm sure."

Nick and Danny put their boards in the water, and themselves belly down on top of them. Fury sat down on the beach near the water's edge, put his surfboard down beside him, and watched his friends paddle out. He sat there staring out into the ocean for a long time while the tide came in. Now, instead of sitting on dry sand, the waves were washing up on him, getting his high-tops and his shorts wet. Still he didn't move. He really didn't *want* to head home. What kind of home was it, anyway? Russ just wanted to get rid of him. That thought depressed Fury as much as the thought of seeing Tracy kissing Will.

Maybe, he'd just sit here, he decided, until the waves completely covered him. That's what he deserved, he thought, for making everyone around him so miserable—and himself, the most miserable of all. How could he have messed things up so badly with Tracy, the only person who even cared if he lived or died? The way his whole summer had turned into one big disaster, it was an even greater wonder to him that he hadn't done something worse! He was up to his waist in water now and the glare of the sun off the ocean hurt his eyes, but still he didn't care. All of a sudden, he spotted a surboard floating out to sea. Where was his board? he asked himself, looking around him. Realizing it was his, Fury dove into the water and swam out after the board. He nabbed it quickly and headed back in. As he dragged it onto shore, it surprised him to discover that he cared enough about his board to even go after it. It was reassuring, in a way.

As Fury came out of the water, he saw Jed walking down the beach toward him.

"I don't blame you for surfing with your shirt and shoes on," Jed commented when he saw Fury. "The sun's real strong at this time of day and I heard some of the rocks out there are pretty nasty."

"Where did you come from?" Fury asked.

"Leslie's tower," Jed answered. "I've got the afternoon off and I came by to say hello to her. Then I thought I'd check out the surfing action and see if I could pick up a few tips. Where are your surfing buddies?"

"Out surfing, where else?"

"Why aren't you surfing with them?"

"I wasn't actually surfing. My board drifted out and I had to dive in to rescue it." Fury was glad that Jed had shown up when he did. Like the board floating out to sea and shaking him out of his deep depression, it was a good omen.

"Oh, that's headline news. I can see it now in the *Marina Bay Beacon.* 'Surfer in Pink High-Tops Rescues Surfboard,'" Jed quipped.

"Don't mention the word 'headline' to me," he scowled, even though he knew that Jed was only trying to make him laugh. It would take a lot of doing on Jed's part, however, to get Fury to even smile.

"Why not?" Jed asked.

"Got time for a long story?" Fury asked, sitting down on the sand farther away from the water this time.

"Sure I've got time. Even if I didn't, I'd make time for you, Fury. What's on your mind?" Jed wanted to know. He dropped himself into the sand next to Fury.

Fury filled Jed in on how he had wrecked Tracy's chances to headline at Nashville Night.

"If you ask me, Will was just looking for an excuse to get out of it," Jed reasoned. "I mean, maybe he had second thoughts about her being a big enough name in the first place. Otherwise, why would he have taken out what *you* said to him on her?" he pointed out. "He didn't have to do that—he probably wanted to."

Fury had to admit that Jed's argument made a lot of sense.

"I know you two pretty well by now," Jed continued. "The bigger the blowup, the better the kiss and makeup."

Fury mustered a weak smile. "Tracy's only one of my worries. There's also the house meeting tonight."

"Relax, Fury. I'm sure nothing will come of it. Maybe Russ is looking for an excuse to get you out, and if he decides to make a big deal of it at the meeting, Leslie won't have much choice but to go along with her brother. But nobody else wants you to leave. Pamela's been away so she has nothing against you. I'm on your side, and I'm sure your own girl friend won't vote against you. If it comes to a vote, it's three to two, you stay," Jed said.

"I wouldn't be so sure about Tracy. This could be her chance to get back at me for ruining her golden opportunity. I wouldn't even blame her if she did want to kick me out," Fury said, feeling depressed.

"Don't be so down on yourself. Things will probably turn out the way you least expect them to. Hey, I'm getting hungry. I think I'll get some lunch on Surfrider. Want to join me?"

"Nah," Fury said, going back to staring out at the ocean again.

"Then I'll see you tonight. Remember—you can count on me for support," Jed reminded him as he started walking away.

"Thanks for trying to cheer me up," Fury called to him. But after what he had done to Tracy, Fury knew that it would be a long time before she forgave him. A *long* time.

Chapter 7

Fury sat on the beach and vegetated all day, until mothers lowered their beach umbrellas and took their tots in tow, teenagers snatched up their beach blankets and boom boxes, and everyone around him packed up their beach gear and started for home. He didn't see Nick or Danny again all day; they'd probably moved farther on down the beach in search of better surf, but that was just as well. He really wasn't in the mood to talk to anyone. He was glad that Jed had come along earlier. He had lifted Fury's spirits a little, and had almost convinced him that the house meeting wouldn't result in disaster. Well, Fury thought, there was only one way to find out; he'd have to head home.

As he hit Surfrider around six o'clock to

thumb a ride, he vaguely remembered that he and Tracy had made a date to meet for dinner to prepare for the house meeting. But Fury was sure that after what had happened this morning, Tracy wouldn't even want him to show up, much less be expecting him.

Around six-thirty Fury finally hitched a ride back to the house. As he was coming up the walk, Pamela pulled up in her blue BMW convertible and beeped her horn at him.

"Do you think you could help me carry my bags?" she asked when he turned around.

"No problem," Fury called down to her. "I'll just put my board in the house and come right back."

Fury returned with his hands free just as Pamela stepped out of her BMW wearing a pair of white crushed-linen slacks, a matching camp shirt, and a pair of white espadrilles that tied around her ankles. Fury walked around to the trunk of her car and took out the two huge suitcases. He knew the routine all too well. He had helped carry Pamela's designer bags up to her room when she had first moved in. He had never known anyone before with so many pieces of luggage, let alone such elegant clothes to go in them. He carried the suitcases up to her room like a well-trained bellboy, half expecting her to tip him, then came downstairs. Pamela thanked him as she headed into the living room to announce to her housemates that she was back in time for the important house meeting.

Fury, meanwhile, ducked into the den before anyone else had a chance to see him.

He needed some time to pull himself together. He fixed his hair in front, then plopped into the beanbag chair to think things through. Jed, Fury realized, was right, as usual. Fury didn't have anything to worry about; Russ would just be going through the motions at the meeting, trying to threaten him. Fury would promise to behave. Couldn't Russ tell from how he'd left the kitchen and bathroom this morning that he was already trying? He'd also promise to look for a new job so he could pay his share of the rent if Russ could just wait a little while longer. Maybe his promise would help his cause with Tracy. In any case, Russ would be hard nosed and ask to take it to a vote. But just as Jed had predicted, Fury would win; he'd been all wrong about Will and Tracy; she was still his girl friend and would fight for him. If it was all going to go so smoothly, then why did it feel like a skateboarder was doing end overs and kick turns in his stomach? The very thought of being in the same room with Tracy made Fury nervous. He couldn't stand the suspense another second. He sprang up from the beanbag chair, certain that he'd rather confront Russ and Tracy than sit in his room and imagine what was going to happen. He checked himself out one last time in the mirror. He knew he looked good.

But when he sauntered into the living room, conversation stopped and all eyes turned to him, and Fury's confidence took a nose dive. He sat down in a stuffed chair by the window without saying anything.

"Everyone's here so we might as well begin," Russ said matter-of-factly.

The way Russ, Leslie, Tracy, Jed, and Pamela were all lined up on the two matching peach sofas across from him made Fury feel as if he were on trial. One by one he panned the faces of his jurors, trying to get a feel for how his case stood with them. When Russ and Leslie caught his gaze they avoided making eye contact with him; Jed, seated next to them, gave him a reassuring thumbs-up sign; and Pamela actually winked at him, something she had never done before. Fury couldn't tell what she meant by it; thanks for helping me with my bags, or something more significant? But Tracy's stare straight past him and out the window was easy to interpret. She was too angry and upset to even look him in the eye.

When Russ began to speak, Fury half-expected him to say, "Do you swear to tell the truth, the whole truth, and nothing but the truth?"

But instead he began, "Okay, you all know why I've called this meeting. I told Pamela on the phone when she called yesterday so I'm not going to beat around the bush. We've got some problems in the house that I think we have to work out. So here's what I'd like us to do. Let's go around the room and get the problems out in the open. I'll go first."

Fury listened intently as Russ, playing the part of the prosecutor to the hilt, spelled out the problems. Fury had heard them all before, from Russ's promise to his parents to take care of the house while they were on vacation, to Fury not paying his rent on time. The only surprise came when Russ concluded, "And when Fury came home plastered, passed out on the deck, and slept there all night, that presented the worst problem of all. All I needed was for the neighbors to have seen him and notified my parents! And they'd do it, too. They threatened to call them in Europe before, when the beach bums were hanging out in front of the house." Russ paused, thought a moment, then continued, "I think I've covered everything. Leslie, you're next."

Fury could tell just from where Leslie was sitting that Russ had set her up. Still, he sensed her discomfort in having to say, "Russ has pretty well covered all of the house problems that I was going to bring up."

It didn't come as a big surprise to Fury that, so far, he was the only house problem under discussion.

"Thanks, Leslie. Jed, you're next," Russ said, apparently happy that the meeting was moving right along.

Jed's big brown eyes widened, and he smiled at Fury. "First of all, I want to clear something up right from the beginning. Russ might have gotten upset when Fury ate my food, but, personally, that kind of thing doesn't present a problem for me," he admitted. "If someone's hungry and I've got some food, I don't mind sharing it. Second of all, the fact that Fury quit his job doesn't mean he can't get another one. And third of all, and this to my mind is my most important point, if someone is having a rough time, I believe you try to *help* him. We're Fury's family, for the summer anyway, and instead of just getting mad at—"

Russ cut Jed off in midsentence. "Your turn, Pamela," he said curtly. Fury couldn't help smiling to himself over what Jed had just said. It made him feel good inside.

"I agree with Jed," Pamela began. "And in all honesty, I haven't been around lately so I really don't have any house problems to bring up. I have enough problems of my own, but this isn't the time or the place to discuss them." Pamela pushed back her straight, brown hair to reveal a solid-gold earring. Fury figured that this was her way of signaling that she was done and that she wasn't going to tell them just what her problems were. He was right. Pamela turned to Tracy, who was sitting next to her, and said, "You can go now, Tracy." All eyes turned toward Tracy. Everyone knew that Fury's fate was in her hands. He looked at her hard, trying to get her to meet his stare. But, once again, she looked straight through him.

Finally, she turned toward him. "Where were

you? I thought I was meeting you after work. I waited over an hour for you."

"After what happened in the cafe, I really didn't think you wanted to see my face!" Fury exclaimed.

"What do you mean? I thought you'd at least have the decency to show up and offer some lame excuse—if not to apologize outright for your outrageous behavior!" Tracy shouted.

"After what you were doing with Will, why should *I* apologize?" Fury retorted.

"Oh, please, Fury—not that again. I told you this morning, we were just doing business!"

"And I know what kind of business," Fury snapped.

"Hey, you two, this is not divorce court," Russ interjected. "We're having a house meeting here. Let's wrap it up and then you can get on with your screaming match."

"This time you've gone too far," Tracy rushed on, ignoring Russ's comments. "After wrecking my chances for Nashville Night, you expect me to apologize to *you*?" She turned to Russ. "I'll be glad to wrap up this meeting for you right now. As far as I'm concerned, the biggest problem in this house is Angelo DeFurie."

"That's it, Fury. You're out, at least until you can get your act together. Meeting adjourned," Russ concluded quickly. He got up from the couch and walked out of the room without even looking at Fury. After Russ left, there wasn't any real reason for Pamela, Jed, or Leslie to hang around, and they quickly got up, looking a little dazed, and left the room.

When everyone except Tracy had gone, Fury couldn't hold back his anger any longer. "Don't think I'm too crushed about having to split." he said to his now ex-girl friend. "I wouldn't want to live under the same roof with a tramp like you."

"Look who's calling *me* names! The original flake, who doesn't even know what day it is! You're incapable of caring about anyone but yourself, you know that?"

"Now look who's talking! You'd do anything to get on stage," Fury yelled back.

"At least I *care* about getting ahead," Tracy objected. "You'd surf your life away if you had the chance."

"And I'm happy to say that starting tomorrow, that's exactly what I plan to do."

"Well, that figures," Tracy said snidely. Then she calmly turned her back on Fury and walked out of the room.

Chapter 8

"Where are you going to stay tonight?" Jed asked as he helped Fury carry his gear out to Jed's van on Saturday morning.

"Hey, man, I'm on top of it. I'll either crash on the beach or Nick or Danny will put me up until I can get it together. Not to worry," Fury told him.

"Well, let me know where you end up so we can stay in touch," Jed said as he unlocked the rear door and loaded Fury's backpack into the van.

Fury tied his skateboard to the top of the pack. "Thanks for storing my bass and amplifier in your room. I'll be back for them as soon as I get settled," he said as he maneuvered his surfboard into the back of the VW.

"No sweat. I'm just sorry that things worked

out this way. I didn't expect you'd really have to move. If there's anything else I can do to help, just holler," Jed said, then came around to the driver's side of the van and got behind the wheel. Fury walked around to the other side and climbed in next to him.

"Thanks for the ride, Jed. Thanks for everything else, too. You're a cool dude," Fury told Jed as he started the engine and pulled away from the curb. Fury never dreamed he'd say anything like that to Jed; but then again, he wouldn't have thought that nerdy, unathletic Jed, of all people, would be the guy to come through for him, either. Well, he had found out the night before who his friends were—and Tracy sure wasn't one of them. Russ and Leslie hadn't turned out to be very friendly, either. To be honest, he wasn't that sorry to be moving on. Why should he hang around with people who didn't appreciate him? But Pamela sure had surprised him, Fury thought, as Jed turned off Sandpiper and onto the highway.

"You can drop me off here," Fury told Jed when they had reached the public par course.

Jed pulled into the parking strip next to an old yellow-and-white VW camper and turned off the engine. Fury got out and unloaded his gear from the back, then walked up to Jed.

"I'll get in touch with you as soon as I find a place to crash," Fury said, extending his hand.

"Thanks. I'd like that. Then you can keep me current on what's happening with you, and I can keep you posted on what's happening around the house," Jed replied, slapping the palm of Fury's hand.

"Sure thing," Fury said, although he wasn't so sure he wanted to know what Tracy would be doing with Will now that he was out of the picture.

Jed pulled away from the parking strip. Fury gathered up his gear, trekked across the grassy par course, and out onto the sandy beach. With his sleeping bag and skateboard lashed onto his pack and his surfboard under his arm, he might have been mistaken for a drifter, but, unlike one, he had a definite plan. He'd stash his gear at the beach bums' campsite for the day and then go look for Nick and Danny. If either one of them could put him up up for the night, he'd come back for his stuff. Otherwise he'd sleep here on the beach. In the meantime, he figured his stuff would be safe.

Fury approached their campsite. Except for a girl with red straggly hair who was stirring the embers of a dying campfire with a piece of driftwood, no one else was around. But the beach bums' sleeping bags, clothes, and empty beer bottles encircled the concrete campfire ring. They were probably already out surfing, Fury thought. He didn't blame them. The weather was picture-postcard perfect, warm and cloudless at ten o'clock. Just as soon as he unloaded his gear and found Nick and Danny,

Fury reminded himself, he'd be out there ripping waves, too.

"Hi," the girl greeted him.

"Hi. Are you going to be around for a while?" Fury asked, figuring she was the girl friend of one of the beach bums.

"I'm not going anywhere. Why?"

"Could you keep an eye on my gear?" Fury asked. He set down his pack in the sand near some other camping equipment.

"What's your name?" she asked.

"Angelo DeFurie. But everyone calls me Fury," he explained.

"I dig the color of your hair, Fury."

"Thanks. I like yours, too. What's your name?"

"Rain," she answered.

Considering how washed out she looked in her gray tank top and faded, torn jeans, Fury thought that the name suited her. The only bright feature about her was her copper-colored hair. She seemed nice enough, though, and Fury felt he could trust her with his gear. "So what do you say, Rain? Do you think you could watch my stuff?"

"No problem. I'll keep my eye on it. But I don't know how long I'll be hanging out here."

"That's cool. Thanks," Fury said as he picked up his surfboard and got ready to leave.

"Maybe I'll see you later. Maybe I won't," Rain said, sounding spaced out. She went back to poking at the fire.

There's no such thing as a bad day at the

beach, Fury said to himself as he took off in search of Nick and Danny. He just had to get last night's fight with Tracy off of his mind. Actually, he felt pretty good about life, in spite of the fact that he'd broken up with his girl friend and had been kicked out of the house. The golden day had put him in a really good mood.

His optimistic outlook only improved when he ran into Danny just a little ways down the beach.

"Hey, man, I've been looking for you," Danny exclaimed, rushing up to him.

"I've been looking for you guys, too. What's up?"

"Nick was talking about heading up to Rincon Beach for the day. He heard the waves are spilling one on top of the other out at the point. So he sent me to look for you. We're supposed to meet him back at his car," Danny said.

"What are we waiting for? Let's cut out!" Fury whooped.

Minutes later, Nick, Danny, and Fury were securing their boards to the top of Nick's restored, '47 Ford and piling into his classic, wood-paneled station wagon.

"I've got a present for you," Nick said, pulling his pink, yellow and, aqua board shorts out of a duffel bag and tossing them into the backseat where Fury was sitting.

"Oh, raw. Thanks, Nick." Fury slid down in the backseat so he wouldn't be seen and quickly slipped out of his old cutoffs and into the coveted board shorts. "Hey, I've got some news for you."

As they cruised up the coast in Nick's car, Fury filled them in on how things were with him and Tracy, and how Russ had booted him out of the beach house. He planned to wait, however, for just the right moment before asking if he could crash at either of their pads tonight.

"Like the looks of your car," a pretty girl with brown, windswept hair and a deep tan shouted at them as she whizzed past them in a green MG convertible.

"Like yours, too," Fury shouted out the back window. He was referring to her good looks, not her car's, not that it really mattered. By then, she was several cars ahead of him and, more than likely, never heard him.

They spent the rest of the trip to Rincon admiring other classy-looking girls and cars and, in turn, being admired, or attempting to tune in stations on Nick's funky old radio and listening to scratchy songs on it.

As they pulled up at the point and Nick parked, the sun sparkled on the water.

"Look at that perfect three-wave set," Fury shouted in anticipation of getting up and under it.

"Yeah. Terrific. But get a load of that busload of kids changing in the parking lot," Nick said, calling Fury's attention to a group of novices swarming around a yellow school bus and slipping into fluorescent-colored wet suits.

"I guess you weren't the only one who heard the surf was awesome at Rincon," Fury grumbled to Nick. Fury, Nick, and Danny stashed their shirts, shoes, and shades in the car, took their boards off the car rack, and bounded down to the beach, wanting to hit the water before the junior pack.

"Go home, gremmies!" Fury shouted over his shoulder as he paddled out. It was hard enough to battle the strong current, and he certainly didn't want to bother with dodging the local novices.

On his first ride, Fury beat the rush. He dropped in on a perfect wave and got tubed all the way into shore. Nick broke to the right, and Danny to the left, and they rode in on the second wave right behind them. They wasted no time paddling out again, trying to keep ahead of the crowd. But just when Fury was up and ready to carve another set of waves, a local gremlin in neon green shouted, "Outside!" and rudely dropped in on Fury's wave, tossing Fury into the falls. Fury came up from under the crashing wave, caught his breath and his flyaway board, and paddled the rest of the way in.

"Let's split," Fury suggested as Nick and Danny beached their boards right after him. "These kids are bigger pests than a flock of hungry sea gulls. Speaking of being hungry, why don't we drive into Santa Barbara and get some fish and chips at the Brown Pelican?"

"You're on!" Danny said.

Nick nodded in agreement. "This place is beat."

The next thing Fury knew, their boards were back on the roof of the car, and with the windows down, they were making their way to the beachside restaurant another fifteen miles up the coast.

Now that they weren't in a big rush to go surfing, Nick drove even slower, allowing them plenty of time to appreciate the warm breezes off the ocean and the scenic views along the coastal highway. Some highway construction as they neared Santa Barbara didn't help them get to their destination any faster; traffic slowed down to a snail's pace as it was diverted into one lane. Fury couldn't wait to get out of the car when they finally pulled up in front of the seaside restuarant.

They walked around the side of the wooden building to the deck in the back and seated themselves around a wooden table with an opened beach umbrella in the center. A waitress came outside and took their order, and ten minutes later they were digging into greasy orders of fish and chips. Fury closed the umbrella to allow the hot, afternoon sun to beat down on them as they ate. It quickly warmed their bare chests and dried their wet board shorts. The moment was right, Fury now thought, to also warm Nick or Danny up to the idea of his crashing at either of their pads.

"Hey, dudes," he began, "You know, I left all

my gear with some girl on the beach back in Marina Bay."

Nick shifted his body in his chair to better catch the rays. Danny popped two more fries into his mouth. Neither one seemed to be wondering what Fury was going to do with his stuff now that he didn't have a room to put it in. Fury had hoped that one of them would have responded with the obvious question, "Where are you going to sleep tonight?" but they left Fury with the task of bringing up the subject himself. "Well, I was wondering," he continued even though he hated the idea of inviting himself, "if maybe one of you could put me up for the night."

Nick sat up in his chair and took off his shades. He looked at Fury sympathetically. "Hey, man, I'm sorry. I wish I could. But I'm really on the outs with my parents. If I were talking to them, I'd be more than glad to ask them if you could stay a couple of nights . . . ."

"That's cool, Nick. You don't have to explain. I understand. I just thought I'd ask. What about you, Danny?"

"I've got a problem at my house, too. The place is crawling with out-of-town guests. I'm sharing my room with my bratty, ten-year-old cousin all next week. I came real close to having to spend today with him, but I lucked out. He wanted to go to Disneyland instead. I'll probably be stuck with him all day tomorrow, though," Danny said.

Fury felt sorry for Danny—but even worse, he felt sorry for himself again. He pushed away his fish and chips, unable to eat any more. Now that he knew the score with Nick and Danny, he had to face the fact that he'd be sleeping on the beach.

The reality of his situation came crashing down on him. He was a beach bum. A drifter. An outcast with no place to go or stay. Old feelings from his childhood of what it was like growing up without parents, of being an orphan, hurtful memories that were buried deep inside him, suddenly came rushing back. He remembered how painful it had been for him and how uprooted he had felt when circumstances had forced him to leave the security of one foster home and go to a new one. But now it was even worse. He had no home, not even a temporary one, to go to.

It was just like him, he now realized, to have made himself unwanted at Russ's house. Thinking back on it now, sometimes the reasons he had to move from one foster home to another were beyond his control, but, more often, he knew, he had been the cause. Why was he dwelling on all this now? There was nothing to be gained by reliving the past, he told himself, especially when his future was even more depressing and uncertain. He was suddenly overcome by the need to unite with his pack and his other few possessions—he had to hang on to something.

"I ought to be heading back into Marina Bay soon. The girl who's keeping an eye on my stuff didn't know how long she'd be hanging out there," Fury explained.

"Why don't we head back now?" Nick obliged. "I've just about had it out in the sun, anyway. I think my brain is getting sunburned."

"I'm ready to split," Danny said, finishing off the last piece of Fury's fish.

On their way back to Marina Bay, Fury felt more like he was riding in a funeral procession than in Nick's '47 classic Ford. As the old Woody station wagon lumbered down the highway going about as fast as a hearse, no one said much; Danny didn't even try to tune in the radio. Everyone seemed lost in his own thoughts. Fury couldn't get his mind off what Jed had said at the house meeting last night, "We're Fury's family, for the summer anyway." Well, now he didn't have any family, not even a surrogate one.

Two hours later, although it felt more like five, as Nick approached the turnoff to the Seahorse Shores complex, he asked Fury, "Where should I drop you off?" Fury almost directed him to Russ's house, but he caught himself and told Nick to continue on to the par-course parking strip. Nick pulled up a couple of cars away from the yellow-and-white VW camper that was still parked there. Fury jumped out of the car and started getting his stuff together.

"Listen, Fury, when I'm on better terms with

my folks, maybe I can ask them if you can stay over," Nick said haltingly.

"Yeah, man, and when my relatives split, I'll ask mine if you can crash at our house," Danny also offered.

"Hey, not to worry, dudes. Everything's cool. I've got things under control. I'm used to living on the edge," Fury assured them as he lifted his board off the car rack. With his big gun under his arm and with as much bravado as he could muster, he waved good-bye to Nick and Danny and took off in the direction of the beach bums' campsite.

He hopped over a couple of balance beams along the par course, then, when he hit the sand, broke into a trot. By the time some people and a couple of pup tents came into Fury's view, he was practically sprinting, running as fast as he could on the sand while he dragged his big board behind him. If he could just keep running, he'd get out of Marina Bay and all of his problems. Fury knew what he had said to Nick and Danny about having everything under control was a lie. Living on the beach out of a pack wasn't living on the edge: It wasn't even living; it was the end of the road.

In spite of his urge to keep on going, Fury slowed down when he reached the campsite. He glanced around, first for Rain, then for his pack. It was obvious to him that she had split; there were only two guys around and they were sitting on the concrete campfire ring with their backs toward Fury and their faces in the sun. From the back neither one looked like Goofy, and Fury was pretty sure he didn't know them. He looked for his pack where he had last put it down, but it wasn't there. Fury hoped that Rain had just tossed it into the jumble of beach bums' packs for safekeeping. He began to rummage through the pile.

"Say, did either of you two dudes see a royal-blue pack with a skateboard tied onto it?" Fury asked them, trying to sound as cool as possible when he didn't find it.

The two guys turned around. One of them, answered, "Can't say that we did." Then they both went back to sunning themselves.

Fury felt a wave of panic sweep over him, the same desperate feeling he had experienced only moments ago as he raced across the beach. But now he understood why he had wanted to keep on running. He had had a funny feeling all along that his pack wouldn't be here. Why did he think it would be? he now asked himself. Hadn't he already lost Tracy, a place to live, everything in his life that was important to him? He kicked the sand, then picked up a thin, smooth rock and threw it in disgust as far out into the ocean as he could. As he watched it skip over the water, then, finally, sink and vanish, he wished, for a moment, that he was that rock.

Chapter 9

Fury frantically searched the camp again, up-ending packs and sleeping bags. He crawled in vain inside the pup tents, and even went so far as to rummage through a nearby litter can in the hope that someone had dumped his pack there as a practical joke. But it was no joke. The pack wasn't in the can, it wasn't anywhere around; it was gone.

Then Fury remembered the yellow-and-white VW camper that he had seen parked at the par course early that morning. It occurred to him that the owner of the camper might have ripped off his pack. That made a lot of sense. The owner had probably seen Fury head out to the beach with it this morning, and had waited, who knows how long, until he figured no one was around. Then, by the time he walked out on the beach, Rain had left; with the beach bums off surfing, the pack would have been his for the taking. It was probably Fury's skateboard with its new red deck, shiny silver trucks, and hot yellow wheels that the guy was really after, but it was just as easy to make off with the entire pack than it was to untie the skateboard from it. All the dude had to do was pick up the pack, put it on his back, walk away with it, and no one would be the wiser. He'd have all the time in the world to remove the skateboard from the pack once he got back inside his camper.

Fury knew that the camper had still been there when Nick had dropped him off. He hoped he could catch up with it.

But by the time he got back to the parking strip, the camper was gone. The thief had disappeared with all of his belongings—as few of them as there were.

If Fury ever had a reason to feel really sad, it was now. He had no home, no girl friend, no pack, and no idea what to do next. He sat down on the asphalt, set his board down beside him, and put his head in his hands. He felt a pain in his chest, and he had to fight back tears. If only he had someone to comfort him . . . and not just anyone. He wanted Tracy.

Fury closed his eyes and imagined Tracy's soft cheek next to his. Then he flashed back to the wild time they had had together riding the roller coaster at the Fun Zone, and some nice moments they had shared practicing for Nashville Night together in his room. If only he could take back all the dumb things he had said and done and hold her in his arms this very minute. He couldn't stand thinking about her; he missed her too much.

But when he recalled the cruel things Tracy had said to him just twenty-four hours ago, Fury didn't feel quite so fond of her. He had to forget about her, they obviously weren't meant to be together. Why did he think he needed her? All she did was complain about him, like everyone else. No, what he needed now was a beer. Recalling an ice chest at the campsite, Fury picked himself up from the asphalt, grabbed his surfboard, and headed back to the beach bums' hangout.

When Fury returned, the same two guys were there. "Did you find your pack?" the one who had spoken to him earlier asked. He and his friend were sprawled out on top of sleeping bags on the sand.

Fury shook his head.

"Man, that's a bummer."

"Yeah, no kidding. I don't really want to talk about it," Fury said. "Now I'm looking for another kind of pack—a six-pack. Got any beer around?"

"Sure, help yourself." The guy pointed to an ice cooler at the foot of his bag. Fury lowered his board to the sand, stepped over to the cooler, and took out two cans of beer.

"Let me contribute a couple of dollars to the cause," Fury offered, taking some bills out of his wallet.

"Thanks. Contributions are always welcome," the talkative guy said as Fury handed him the money.

Fury sat down in the sand near the two guys. He wasted no time in opening the first beer and drinking almost all of it in one gulp. After a few minutes, when he began to feel the heady effects of the alcohol, he wanted to strike up a conversation. Although he didn't know either of these guys, at least the talkative one seemed pretty friendly. Fury had a hunch that he could tell his troubles to him.

"Hey, I bet you wouldn't believe that besides someone stealing my pack, I got kicked out of the house I was living in *and* my girl friend broke up with me, all in less than twenty-four hours. How's that for bum luck?" Fury said, looking for some company, if not sympathy.

But obviously he had come to the wrong place for either one. The beach bums, these two at least, weren't as friendly as Fury had remembered them. "Look, buddy, I don't mind sharing some beer with you, but I don't want to hear your life story. We're all down and out around here," the seemingly friendly guy said. "Now if you don't mind I think I'll catch a few zees."

Picking up his next can of beer, Fury stood up and walked down toward the water. He hoped that he hadn't gotten a sample of what living on the beach with guys like these would be like.

Fury plopped himself down in the sand again to savor the second beer and the still-warm late-afternoon sun. He downed this can slowly, hoping the alcohol would deaden his memory. What he couldn't remember couldn't hurt him. But the beer didn't get him high fast enough and he began to think about what a rotten life he'd had. He recalled how he had always felt lonely in the foster homes he had lived in as a child, the way he did now—he had never had someone who made him feel loved. But that intense lonely feeling had left him when he met Tracy. And now, having only himself to blame, the best thing that had ever happened to him was gone. He sure had a knack for screwing up his life. He picked up his beer can and emptied it, not wanting to review his mile-long list of past and present screwups. Finally, he felt better, and the pain went away. He was so relaxed that he felt sleepy. He stretched out on the sand and closed his eyes.

Fury didn't even hear Rain come up to him, but all of a sudden she was shaking him by the shoulder, trying to wake him up. "C'mon, I've got your pack in my car," she said. "Come *on*."

Fury was just awake enough to realize that she wasn't joking. He grabbed his surfboard and followed her back to the parking strip. But he thought he must be dreaming when she opened the rear door of the yellow-and-white VW camper and showed him the proof. There it was, his royal-blue pack, with his brown sleeping bag and red skateboard lashed to it.

"This is your camper?" Fury asked Rain, not really understanding what had just happened.

"Yes. This is my camper and this is your pack," she replied, pointing to them and speaking slowly, as if English was his second language.

"Okay. I get it. But let me ask you one more dumb question. *Why* is my pack in your camper?"

"Well, I was going to leave it on the beach when I had to go. But then I got to thinking that I said I would watch it. I didn't know when you would be coming back here so I took it with me. I figured it was safer with me than on the beach. Come to think of it, I could say the same about *you*. You look pretty bent. Do you want to crash in my camper tonight?"

"Out of sight! That's really nice of you. Are you sure you have enough room?" Fury asked politely, not wanting to take Rain's offer for granted.

"Sure. The seat pulls out and turns into a double bed," Rain replied.

Fury didn't want to dwell on the implications of Rain's explanation about the bed. Besides, even if he thought about it, he was too bombed to care. All that seemed important to him now was that his pack was safe and he had a place to sleep.

"Get in," Rain said, obviously assuming that Fury was planning to spend the night. "I don't like to park the camper here overnight. About a half an hour from here up the coast there's a public campground with electricity and showers and stuff. I usually make that my home away from home," she explained.

Although Fury had never stayed there overnight, he knew the campground. It was about a twenty-minute walk or ten-minute drive from the Seahorse Shores complex. A couple of weeks ago, when the word was out that it was a big-wave weekend at Hollister, Fury, Nick, and Danny had caught a boat ride from the foot of the pier at the campground and braved an eight-mile run up the coast to the great-wave beaches at Hollister Ranch. Catching a boat ride from the campground was the only way to reach The Ranch without trespassing.

Fury stood on the runner of the camper and hoisted his surfboard on top of the car. Then he secured it with some rope that was tied to the roof rack. "Where is home?" he asked as he climbed back down and into the front seat.

"Washington. But I haven't lived up there in years. It rains too much."

"That's pretty funny. Your name's Rain, but you don't like the rain," Fury commented as she started the car.

"Yeah. I like it every once in a while, but not

when it rains nine months out of the year the way it does in Washington. My mother likes to tell the story of how it rained the whole time while she was pregnant with me. So when I was born, she just decided to name me Rain," she recounted, as she backed out of the parking strip.

In no time at all they were out on the highway and Fury was passing the entrance to the Seahorse Shores complex for the second time that day. He had to make a conscious effort not to think about Tracy. Instead he tried to focus on how nice Rain—someone who'd only known him for a few minutes—was being.

"What about you? Where do you make your home?" Rain finally asked, as they pulled into the campground. It was dark by then, and the ranger at the park entrance was already off duty. Rain stopped the car and got out. She picked up an envelope, deposited the nightly campsite fee in it, and then dropped the envelope into a special collection box. When she climbed back in, she'd already forgotten the question she'd asked Fury, and he didn't go out of his way to remind her. Talking about where he lived was never one of his favorite subjects—not now, for sure.

"Well, here we are. Home sweet home," Rain said as they drove into a vacant campsite. She turned off the ignition and set the emergency brake. They both got out of the camper, and Rain busied herself for the next few minutes making camp. Taking an extension cord out of one of the cabinets, she plugged one end into an electrical outlet inside the camper. As soon as she plugged the other end into an exterior electrical outlet at the campsite, the interior of the camper was flooded with warm light. Then she slid the side and back checkered curtains closed. She even had one that snapped on and covered the front window. Out of another cabinet she removed her sleeping bag, then directed Fury to get his from the back. When Fury got out his bag, he tossed it to Rain, who lowered the bed and spread out their bags, side by side.

"Isn't this cozy?" Rain asked after she was done transforming her VW from a passenger car into a cabin for two.

Fury nodded. Picturing himself sleeping right next to Rain, Fury thought it was very cozy, indeed. He certainly had to admit that it was a lot more comfortable and neater looking than some of the pads he had lived in up in San Francisco.

"Why don't you climb in, and we can talk and get to know each better?"

By now it was dark and chilly outside, and Rain's little sleeping space was so warm and inviting that Fury didn't need Rain to coax him inside. As they stretched out next to each other on their sleeping bags, the only place to really get comfortable, Fury wondered if Rain had something other than talk in mind. She was kind of cute in her own washed-out way, and if she did want to make out with him, well, Fury might just be too drunk to put up much of a protest. And why should he? Who knew what could develop? he wondered, toying with the idea that she might even turn out to be the right girl for him. But she quickly made Fury realize that his romantic reverie was only wishful thinking when she said, "You never really told me where you're from. Are you from around here?"

"No, I'm from up north, San Francisco, but the surf's really cold up there in summer, so I thought I'd head south, see what it was like down here," he mumbled.

"I know what you mean. It's worse in Washington. So how do you like it down here?"

"I like it." It amazed Fury how he could carry on such a lighthearted conversation after all he'd been through recently. But the beer had created the temporary impression that his life was looking up. And actually, as he looked over and smiled at Rain, he had to admit that the situation *did* look pretty good.

"So, what do you do up north all year?"

"Well, during the day I'm a bicycle messenger, except that I usually use my skateboard instead of riding one of those clunky, thick-tired bikes messengers usually use. And at night I play backup bass—when I can get a gig, that is. What about you, what do you do?" Fury asked her.

"Not much. You know, I'm getting tired. I think I'll go wash up and get ready for bed. Want to come? The washrooms are just a little way off.

I've got a flashlight," she said, removing it from a small closet and turning it on. From the same closet she pulled out a towel and a cosmetic bag. Then she signaled Fury with her flashlight to come along.

Fury decided not to pursue the issue. He knew that when he avoided a question, it was usually because he had a good reason not to answer it. Rain probably didn't do much of anything, Fury figured. And that was certainly no problem, as far as he was concerned. If she didn't want to talk about her life, then he wouldn't have to talk about his.

Yes, he thought, as he followed her down the paved path to the washrooms, a no-questions-asked relationship with Rain definitely had possibilities.

Chapter 10

Fury bolted upright out of his sleep and hit his head on something unfamiliar. "What's happening?" he wondered aloud, feeling totally disoriented.

"It's just a train. It runs on a high trestle right above the campground. It's early. Go back to sleep, Fury," a woman next to him explained.

A train? Where was he? Who was talking to him? Now Fury was more confused than ever. He rubbed the sleep out of his eyes and took a few minutes to collect his thoughts. When he was awake enough, and his eyes had adjusted to the dark, he could make out his sleeping bag in a camper. Now he remembered where he was. Rain was sleeping beside him. He looked above him and saw that he had bumped his head on a cabinet. Those mysteries solved, he looked over at Rain sleeping peacefully again and wondered how he had ended up spending the night in her camper. He had a hangover and wasn't clear-headed enough to quite figure it all out, but he was reassured to see that they had both slept in their clothes. In all likelihood, nothing had happened between them.

He pulled back a curtain and peeked outside. The sky was just becoming light. Fury thought about getting up and leaving; he could add this experience up to the list of big mistakes he seemed to be so good at making lately. But, Fury leveled with himself as he wriggled back down into his sleeping bag to go back to sleep. He knew he had nowhere else to go.

The sound of sizzling bacon and the smell of fresh coffee awakened Fury later in the morning. He popped up in bed, careful not to knock his head this time. Rain was standing beside the pull-out bed. Fury watched her take the bacon out of the frying pan, put it on a paper plate, and crack four eggs into the bacon grease in the pan. She seemed to Fury to be as at home cooking breakfast on her little built-in stove as she might have been in a full-sized kitchen.

"How do you want your eggs?" she asked when she noticed that Fury was up. "Is over easy okay?"

"Sure," he said, and smiled at her. It wasn't every day that someone served him breakfast in bed. "Anything I can do to help?"

"Why don't you turn the bed back into a seat so we can eat breakfast on it?" Rain suggested.

Fury reached into his back pocket for a comb and made an attempt to spike his unruly hair. When he thought it looked at least as good as Rain's—which wasn't saying much—he scooted out of the bag and slipped on his high-tops.

He pushed the sleeping bags into the rear of the camper and the bed back into a seat while Rain transformed the kitchen into a dining room by swinging a tabletop into place. Next, she set their bacon and eggs on it along with two cups of freshly brewed coffee. As she and Fury sat down to a hungry man's breakfast inside the cozy camper, he couldn't help marvel at the versatility of the vehicle. In fact, he was thinking that the same thought could apply to Rain. She seemed to know exactly what to do to make the camper her permanent home.

"What do you feel like doing today?" Rain asked.

"Do you think you could drive me over to where I used to live? It's only about ten minutes from here. I left my bass guitar and amplifier there." As long as they were in agreement about him staying around for a while and as long as the campsite was equipped with electricity, Fury figured he might as well move all his stuff in and make himself really comfortable. It would be fun, he thought, to sit around a campfire and play some tunes for Rain tonight. While he was at the house, he'd also have a chance to tell Jed where he was staying.

"That's cool. I play a little bass, too. We can drive over and pick it up after breakfast," Rain concurred.

When they were done, Fury offered to help clean up, but Rain insisted that there wasn't enough room in the camper for more than one cook. While she did the dishes, Fury decided to go for a walk on the beach to stretch his legs.

He headed down to the wide, sandy cove, feeling totally in tune with nature. The sun was bright, but the wind was blowing slightly. He liked how it felt on his face. Living right on the beach with Rain was an okay idea, Fury concluded. He stopped to watch the surf break around an offshore oil rig and some brown pelicans skim the ocean in search of breakfast, then continued on toward the pier.

Even before he stepped onto the pier, he spotted several boats out on the water with surfboards jutting out of them. That, Fury knew, meant only one thing: the surf was up at The Ranch. He had to call Nick right away. Surfing at Rincon yesterday had been a big bust, but it would be far less crowded at the Hollister Ranch. Fury was sure that Nick would go for the idea; Danny, however, was stuck baby-sitting his cousin all day. Only the more experienced surfers were willing to put up with a rough boat ride just to get there. Maybe Rain could come along, for the ride. She seemed adept at so many things—maybe, for all Fury knew, she was a surfer herself.

He hurried back to the camper, hoping that Rain had finished the chores. He'd even insist on helping her, he decided, if she hadn't. But Fury's good luck was running in streaks. She had not only finished, but the camper had been converted back to a car and Rain was behind the wheel, ready to roll. Fury climbed in and Rain backed out of the campsite.

"What a great day!" Fury exclaimed as they took off. The excitement of how he planned to spend the day in addition to the thrill of stepping right out of the camper into the bracing fresh air and sunshine had really started his adrenaline flowing.

"Don't you ever get sick of all this sunshine?" Rain inquiried. "Sometimes I wish it would rain."

"Don't *say* that, Rain!" Fury exclaimed, laughing. "Don't even *think* it. The only time I want to hear that word mentioned is when I say your name."

"I'm just kidding, stupid. I love this weather. That's why I moved down here. It's like one long endless summer. Every day when I wake up, the only thing I have to decide is whether I want to go swimming, windsurfing, or just hang out on the beach all day. Speaking of tough decisions like those, what should we do after we pick up your bass?" Rain asked as she turned out of the campground and onto the highway. "It's so gorgeous out."

"I've got it all planned. We can catch a boat from the campground to Hollister and surf The Ranch. Have you ever been out there?"

"No. But I hear it's great."

"Great isn't the word for it. It's awesome. Do you surf?"

"I'm not too bad. I can't do anything fancy, like hang ten, but I can catch a wave and hang on. I'm sure you can teach me what I don't know. I'm especially responsive to the hands-on approach," Rain said flirtatiously.

Heading down the highway, Fury's heart began to pound. He wished he could attribute its quickening to what Rain had just said. But, as they turned into the Seahorse Shores complex, Fury realized why it had been so important for him to pick up his bass today: He wanted Tracy to see him with Rain. He couldn't believe how his mind could play such dirty tricks on him! He didn't really want his bass and amp; he wanted to make Tracy jealous. And, to be up front about it, he knew deep down that he wanted her back.

"Pull up behind that blue BMW convertible," Fury instructed Rain as they neared Russ's house.

"Need any help?" she offered as Fury got out of the car.

"I'll be okay," he lied. He slipped on his shades and raked his hair back, trying to look cool, but his heart was still racing. All he needed now was for Tracy to answer the door. He took a deep breath and rang the bell.

Fury's streak of good luck ran out. Tracy opened the door. Caught unprepared, Fury didn't know what to say. After their big blowup the day before yesterday, he felt very awkward just seeing her. He stood in the doorway for a moment without saying anything.

"Yes? What can I do for you?" Tracy finally asked, as if she were greeting a door-to-door salesman. Fury could tell that it wasn't exactly a comfortable moment for her, either.

"I hope I didn't disturb you. I came to pick up my amplifier and bass," he explained almost apologetically.

"Who's the chick in the car?" Tracy asked, catching a glimpse of Rain in the camper, and changing the tone of their stilted conversation dramatically.

"Oh, just a friend."

"A friend, or a girl friend? You sure don't waste any time playing the field, Angelo De Furie," Tracy commented, making a point of using his full name, which she knew he hated.

"I learned how from you, Tracy Berberian," Fury shot back. "Anyway, what's it to you?"

"Actually, it's nothing to me. I don't know why I'm even bothering to talk to you. Why don't you just come on in and get what you came for?"

Tracy stepped aside brusquely to let Fury pass by. In spite of what she'd just said, he knew he had made her angry, and possibly jealous, too. But it hadn't been worth it. Just seeing Tracy again turned his stomach inside out. He bolted upstairs to the safety of Jed's room. He was happy to find Jed in his room reading a book—luckily, Jed's roommate, Russ, was nowhere in sight.

"I hope I'm not disturbing you. I came to pick up my bass and amp," Fury announced.

"Not at all. Hey, Fury, it's good to see you. Where are you staying?" Jed asked, putting down his book.

"With a friend."

"Nick or Danny?" Jed asked.

"Nah, another friend. You don't know her." Fury shrugged.

"Oh?" Jed said, his eyes widening as big as his mouth. "Where?"

Although he had done nothing to be ashamed of, suddenly Fury felt embarrassed about answering. This wasn't at all how he, Mr. Cool, thought he'd handle the situation. Coming back to the house had seemed an easy enough thing to do when he had suggested it to Rain. But now, after his encounter with Tracy and Jed, Fury realized that he had returned to the house too soon.

"C'mon, Fury, you can tell me," Jed coaxed.

"In her camper at the campground just down the road," Fury mumbled.

"Oh," Jed said again. "No, really, Fury. I'm glad you told me. Someone ought to know where you are."

"Well, now you know. I've got to get going. She's waiting for me in her camper."

"Can I give you a hand?" Jed offered.

"That would be cool. Thanks, Jed. Oh, wait a sec. I wanted to make a call. Can I use your phone?"

"Be my guest. I'll carry your amp out for you."

While Jed headed downstairs, Fury picked up the phone on Jed's desk and dialed Nick's number.

"Hello?"

"Hey, Nick. This is Fury. The waves must be outrageous at The Ranch. The boats are lined up at the campground almost the length of the pier! I met this girl last night and I thought it would be fun to take her to Hollister today. Want to go with us?" Fury asked his friend.

"Who's the girl?" Nick asked.

Fury couldn't believe that Nick, who normally went crazy whenever he heard that the surf was up, and utterly berserk if it was hot at Hollister, even cared about the company.

"I don't have time to tell you now," Fury informed him. "You'll find out when you meet her. We've got a boat to catch if we want to surf paradise! Now where should we meet?"

As Nick outlined a plan to meet them at the campground pier, Jed returned and whispered, "Hey, Fury. You'd better get your butt out of here. Your 'friend' is getting hot under the collar." he reported.

"Nick, I've got to split. I'll see you in about

thirty mintues," Fury told his friend. Hanging up
the phone, he turned to say good-bye to Jed.

"I'm glad you came by," Jed said. "Take it
easy."

"Yeah. You, too. See you around," Fury said as
he picked up his bass and headed to the front
door. Just as he opened it and was about to
leave, Tracy stepped out of the downstairs
bathroom and walked closer.

"Did you find a place to stay last night?" she
asked.

"I thought what I did meant nothing to you,"
Fury answered, not masking his hurt feelings. If
Tracy still cared for him, if there was any chance
of mending the rift between them, if she was
really interested in how he was doing, now was
her chance to say so, Fury said to himself.

"I'm sorry I asked," Tracy replied, on the
defensive again.

"I've got to go. Nice talking to you," Fury said
sarcastically and walked down to the camper.
Tracy slammed the door behind him. Fury
opened the rear door and slid his bass in next to
his amp. Then he came around the side of the
camper and climbed in.

"What took you so long? Did that girl at the
door detain you?" Rain asked in an agitated
voice.

Fury couldn't believe it! Now Rain was jealous
of Tracy! Somehow, although it hadn't been his
plan, he had managed to make them jealous of
each other. Fury didn't like the tone in Rain's

voice, but he decided to let it slide for the moment. "I was talking to my friend Jed. And I had to make a phone call," he explained.

"For someone who's living out of a backpack, you sure have a lot of friends," Rain remarked. This time she sounded as if she was outright jealous of all of Fury's acquaintances.

"Well, you know the old saying: You can't be too rich or have too many friends. That's why I'm glad I met you," Fury replied, trying to smooth things over between them.

He seemed to have said the right thing. Rain smiled and said sweetly, "Okay, where to now?"

"Back to the campground. We're supposed to meet Nick at the pier in thirty mintues."

"Nick? Who's Nick?" Rain asked, sounding impatient.

"My surfing buddy. He's the guy I just called."

"I wasn't interested in spending the day with your buddy Nick. I thought we'd be together today. Thanks a lot for including me in your special plans." Rain started the engine and pulled sharply away from the curb. When she hit the highway, she drove faster than she had before, as if she was taking her frustrations out on the gas pedal.

It was obvious to Fury that he had said the wrong thing this time. "Hey, take it easy, Rain. I didn't think you'd mind if I invited my buddy. He's a nice guy. He wants to meet you," Fury explained, trying to calm her down. But from the way she accelerated even more, Fury knew he hadn't succeeded. She didn't say another word to him until she pulled into their campsite from the night before.

"Look, Fury, let's get something straight. I thought I'd be spending the day alone with you. Get it? So count me out. You can go play with your friend without me," she said, obviously still annoyed. "Three's a crowd."

Fury couldn't figure where she got off being so angry at him. It wasn't as if he was trying to dump her. He had included her in his plans from the start. If anyone should be angry, he should. He'd only met her yesterday and she was already acting as if she owned him. Maybe, he decided, it was just as well that they would be spending the day apart.

"What are you going to do all day?" he asked, mildly curious.

"I'll find something to do. Would you mind if I played your guitar?"

"Of course not, go ahead." Fury was glad he had his bass to bargain with.

"What time do you think you'll be back?" Rain asked as Fury took his surfboard off of the roof of the camper.

"Oh, the boats start heading back from Hollister around five o'clock, six the latest."

"Well, don't rush back on my account. As long as I can mess around with your bass, I'll be fine here," Rain said, in a somewhat more reasonable tone of voice.

"We can sit around a campfire, and I'll play

you some tunes when I get back," Fury suggested.

"Sounds nice," Rain murmured.

Fury could tell that her thoughts were already on something else, but he wasn't bothered by her less-than-enthusiastic response. He hoisted his board under his arm and turned toward the ocean to check the swells. As he watched a surfer slide the near-perfection waves, he couldn't wait to get to Hollister.

Even if the water was choppy, the boat ride there would seem smooth, compared with the upsetting trip he had just taken back to the house. He desperately wanted to ride the waves at The Ranch and to forget his run-ins with Tracy and Rain. After being harassed by both of them, he didn't want to have to think about either of them all day. And once his board hit the water, he knew he wouldn't give Tracy or Rain a second thought. The only thing that would be on his mind was whether to break to the left or right of a wave.

Chapter 11

"Great. You're here!" Nick called out as Fury came running down the pier toward him. "There's a boat just about to leave."

Fury and Nick raced up a gangplank and into the thirty-footer called *The Sea Spray*. Powered by a small diesel engine, the boat could carry up to twenty passengers. As they climbed aboard, Fury saw that it was almost completely filled with salty, experienced surfers. He and Nick stowed their surfboards in the center of the boat with the others and sat down on a long bench covered with blue flotation cushions.

"Where's your friend?" Nick shouted to Fury over the din of the engine.

"She decided not to come!" Fury yelled back.

"Oh, too bad. I wanted to meet her. What happened?"

The boat headed out to sea, and the sea spray in their faces, combined with the engine noise, prevented Fury from giving Nick an answer. He was grateful for the excuse not to have to explain the circumstances to Nick. Besides, as the boat rocked over the waves to get beyond the point where they broke, it was all Fury could do to keep from getting seasick. Now he remembered why only the hale and hearty surfed Hollister.

Once they were beyond the swells, the sea was not at all rough; the boat steadied out, and although he still couldn't talk to Nick without shouting, Fury could at least enjoy the ride. He took off his shirt to catch the hot, high-noon rays. Out on the ocean with only blue sky and water as far as the eye could see, he felt cut off from civilization, and better yet, from all his petty, everyday problems, Tracy and Rain high on the list among them.

This is the life, he thought. He leaned his head back on the gunwale to get more sun in his face. The gentle rolling of the boat made him drowsy. He felt relaxed and peaceful, like a baby being rocked to sleep in a cradle.

Fury didn't want anything to sidetrack him from spending as much time as possible on the water. It had not been in his original plan to get so bogged down with girls, a job, responsibility. If he had wanted all that, he could have stayed up north. He was glad that Rain had decided not to come along and that he could spend the whole day surfing with his buddy Nick.

He was feeling so serene and laid back that he almost resented it when the mate announced that they had reached The Ranch. As he came around to collect the fares, he reminded the surfers to meet the boat around five o'clock at the same spot it had dropped them off. Fury took out his wallet and handed the mate five dollars. Then he took off his high-tops and shades and stuffed them and his wallet inside his sneakers.

The procedure was to leave your possessions on board, then drop into the water with only your surfboard. That, Fury knew, was the easy part. The tricky part was meeting the boat later, especially if the ocean got rough. Since the boat couldn't come any closer into shore without risking going aground, it was that rendezvous that separated the old salts from the novices, and, in fact, added to the afternoon's excitement. But for now, Fury looked forward to dropping into the water, then in on his first wave.

As Fury stood up on his board with Nick just a wave behind him, he thought that the only thing more beautiful than the sun-drenched day itself was the isolated stretch of sandy beach ahead of him. No blankets, beach umbrellas, or litter dotted the unspoiled shore—only a dozen or so surfers in brightly colored board shorts preparing to paddle out again.

Fury and Nick danced, shredded, ripped, and thrashed on perfect waves all day. It was one of those special surfing days that Fury would get stoked on just recalling. He'd have this day to remember whenever he was landlocked—not that he planned on letting that happen very often. Boy, was he glad that he had quit his lifeguard job. Instead of sitting in a chair all summer, now he could grab a day like this for himself whenever he wanted to. The only thing that was wrong with the day was that it was over much too soon.

When Fury saw the other surfers making the one-way trip to the area where the boat would meet them, he knew it was time to go. He signaled to Nick and with their bellies on their boards, they paddled out beyond the soup. With the other surfers, they floated on their boards as they waited for *The Sea Spray*. The first five minutes Fury was as calm as the ocean; he stretched out on his longboard, belly up, to catch the last of the late-afternoon rays. But when the sun began to bother his eyes, he sat up and anxiously looked around for the boat. He noticed that some of the other surfers were acting restless, too, jumping off and on their boards, scanning the horizon, talking nervously to each other.

Nick paddled over to Fury "What will we do if the boat doesn't show up?" he asked.

"Relax," Fury told Nick. "It'll show up. And if it doesn't, the worst that can happen is that we have to sleep on the beach overnight."

"That could be fun," Nick said.

"Eventually someone will come to get us. they have to—we paid for a round-trip ticket."

Nick grinned appreciatively. Fury's attempt to make light of the situation appeared to have made him feel less anxious. Fury smiled back at him, but underneath he wasn't feeling nearly as self-assured as he was pretending to be.

When Rain had asked him what time he'd be back, Fury had said between five and six o'clock. For all he knew, if he didn't show, she'd get ticked off at him again and do something impulsive like take off with his bass, his amp, all his other stuff—maybe she'd just disappear.

After how strangely she had acted this morning, he really couldn't predict what Rain would do. He'd only met her yesterday, and he really didn't know her all that well. The more that he thought about it, the more he wouldn't put it past her to just take off and leave him high and dry. Maybe she never even had any intention of waiting for him today—it wouldn't matter if he came back or not. She could make off with everything he owned whenever she felt like it. It all made sense now; why she had cooperated with him about picking up the bass; why she had made such a stink about Nick; why she had asked him what time he was coming back. What a fool he'd been! She had even admitted to him that she played the bass!

The wind picked up and Fury began to shiver. Where was the boat? *Maybe this isn't the life,* Fury thought anxiously. Having a steady job and a roof over his head began to look almost appealing. If the boat came in the next few minutes, Fury promised himself that he'd go job-hunting the next morning. This carefree life was turning out to be just the opposite, and Fury had had enough!

Relax, dude, he said to himself. *There's no need to do anything that drastic. You're letting your fears run away with you. The boat will be along any minute. You'll be back at the campground before you know it. Everything will be all right; everything, including Rain's camper, will be there.*

"Maybe we should head back to shore. I'm getting cold," Nick complained, apparently feeling the drop in temperature, too.

Fury looked around to see what the other surfers were doing. Some of them had formed a circle with their boards and seemed to be discussing what to do next.

"Let's find out what the other surfers are doing," Fury suggested.

Nick nodded in agreement. They paddled over and joined the huddle.

"I'm getting nervous," one older-looking surfer said. "I don't like waiting in these kelp beds. The sharks feed on them."

"If we don't get picked up soon, they'll feed on us!" someone shouted out.

The older surfer looked a little worried. He glanced at his waterproof Casio. "If the boat doesn't come in ten minutes, I say we swim into shore."

"What about the locals who patrol the beach at night?" another surfer asked. "I've heard some of them are armed and that they don't give surfers an especially warm reception."

"Let's not panic. We'll worry about that if the boat doesn't show up," the older surfer said. "But I have a feeling it will be along any minute."

As the surfer spoke, Fury started shaking uncontrollably. He didn't think he could stay in the water another second. "I've got to go in. I'm really cold," Fury informed Nick through chattering teeth.

"What about the locals?" Nick asked.

"If I don't go in now, I'll freeze to death here," Fury said and started paddling in toward shore.

"Hey, you guys, the boat's coming!" the older-looking surfer shouted to them when they were almost halfway in.

As he and Nick paddled back frantically, Fury's arm felt a lot like rubber. However, his worst fear—that the two of them would be left behind—fueled him forward. Fortunately, they made it in time. The older-looking surfer helped lift Fury out of the water and over the side of the boat.

Once all the surfers were safe on board, the

mate handed out blankets to those who needed
them, Fury among them, and explained, "The
captain wants to apologize for the delay. Some
seaweed got caught in our cool-water intake
and we had to cut our speed. We'll have to take
it easy on the way back."

As long as he had a blanket around him, Fury
didn't care how fast they went. The only thing
that mattered to him now was that he was out of
the water. But just as soon as he felt warm again,
he was haunted by his old worry. What would he
do if he couldn't find Rain at the campground, if
she had left with all his stuff and without him?
To add to his anxiety, at the speed the boat was
going, Fury thought they'd never get back to the
pier. He'd be so late getting back, Rain would
have even more reason to split without him.
Maybe it would be just as well if he never
returned, he thought, dreading the prospect of
finding a place to sleep that night. Maybe he'd
be better off if he drifted in the sea forever. But
fifteen minutes later the campground pier came
into view. When the boat finally docked, Fury
couldn't get off it fast enough.

"I need you to do me a big favor, Nick," Fury
said as he threw off the blanket and tugged on
his T-shirt and high-tops. "Come with me over
to the campsite where I'm staying."

"Sure. Why?"

"Just come with me. I'll explain later," Fury
said. He snatched up his surfboard, flew down
the gangplank, and across the hard-packed sand

toward Rain's campsite at the far end of the beach, with Nick following closely behind. Even before Fury reached the section of the campground where the RVs were allowed to park, he slowed to a fast walk and breathed a sigh of relief. He could see Rain's distinctive yellow-and-white VW pulled up in her campsite in the distance.

"So, what gives?" Nick asked, catching up to Fury.

"Oh, no biggie. I just had a funny feeling when we were in the water that Rain had taken off with all my stuff. I guess it was just part of my general panic," Fury explained as they arrived at the camper.

"Well, you can breathe easy now," Nick commented. All of Fury's gear, the amp and bass included, were piled up on the ground outside the camper.

Fury looked at his stuff, wondering why it wasn't inside. But then, he told himself, Rain had probably moved it outside in order to neaten up the camper. Why was he always so paranoid about her?

Suddenly the side door of the camper slid open. A guy Fury had seen at the beach bums' camp the day before, stepped out.

"Rain told me to tell you you've been replaced. So collect your stuff and start moving," he said in a rough voice.

"Tell him thanks for letting me play his bass!" Rain called out from inside the camper.

"She told me to tell you thanks for . . ."

"I heard her," Fury said, cutting off the beach bum.

"And tell him that I'm sorry I won't be able to hear him play tonight. But he really bummed me out," she explained.

"Tell her to tell me herself," Fury shouted back, as angry with himself as he was with Rain. All he could think about now was how dumb he'd been to trust her, a perfect stranger, just because she had been a little nice to him. And he hadn't trusted his girl friend, Tracy.

The beach bum made an angry move toward Fury to indicate that he'd better not talk to Rain like that; this was his territory now. Fury made a countermove that told the guy if he was looking for trouble, he was ready for a fight.

"C'mon, Fury, cool it," Nick said. He put down his surfboard, picked up Fury's pack, and hoisted it on his back. "Let's get out of here while you and your stuff are all in one piece."

"You'd better listen to your friend," the guy threatened.

"I'll carry the amp. You take your bass," Nick instructed him.

Fury slung the strap of his bass case around him and his surfboard over his shoulder, giving the bum one last angry look.

He smiled at Fury, climbed back into the camper, and slammed the door shut.

Nick started walking back toward the pier where he had parked his car. "Good thing I came along. Now I know why you wanted me to," Nick commented when Fury caught up with him.

"Yeah. Good thing," Fury said, still frustrated by the way Rain had treated him.

They walked in silence until they reached the parking lot. Then they loaded Fury's gear into Nick's showy station wagon and secured their boards to the top of it.

"So. What's your next move?" Nick asked, breaking the silence.

"You tell me," Fury said, leaving his friend plenty of time to invite him to stay with him.

"I'll tell you what," Nick replied. "I'll ask my mother if you can stay at our house for a while, but you'd better offer to pay for your room and board. Then I think she might go for it."

"Thanks a lot, Nick. You're one rad dude."

Nick unlocked his door and got into the car. Then he reached across the front seat and unlocked Fury's.

"Good thing we got in some decent surfing this afternoon. I guess I'll have to start looking for a job tomorrow," Fury admitted, getting into the car.

"Why don't you get a nighttime job? Nick suggested. "Then it won't cut into your surfing time."

"Cool idea. Thanks, Nick."

"No problem. That's what good friends are for," Nick said as they pulled out onto the highway.

"Yeah," Fury agreed. "That's what good friends are for."

Rain, he now realized, had given him a crash course on friends: how to tell the good ones from the fair-weather ones, the ones you could trust from the ones you couldn't.

Fury wondered what kind of friend *he* was. Thinking back to his experience at the beach house, Fury wasn't so sure he had been a good friend—to anyone. Maybe it was time to work on changing that.

Chapter 12

"Rise and shine. Time for today's singing surf report: They'll be surfing at Rincon, Ventura County line, San Onofre, and Sunset. . . ." Fury opened his eyes and looked at the radio. He had been sound asleep until Nick blasted his boom box. Then he realized it wasn't the radio—Nick was singing the Beach Boys' famous song right in his ear. Fury rolled over on his side.

"But I don't care because I'm surfing Zuma all day!" Nick continued. "Danny called. He said that the waves there are crashing like waterfalls. What about you, Fury? Huh? Are you coming? Huh?!" Nick teased, trying to get his sleepy friend to wake up.

"Cut it out, Nick. I'm awake. What time is it, anyway?" Fury opened his eyes and looked around, half-expecting to see a freestanding fireplace, a beanbag chair, all the familiar furnishings in his old room in Russ's house. Instead, he saw Nick's Jimmy Z surfing posters plastered all over the walls.

"Time to go surfing, pal," Nick said. "I'm supposed to pick Danny up in front of the Surfrider Cafe in fifteen minutes. Then we're zooming down to Zuma. You're up, the surf's up, so let's get moving!"

Fury wasn't sure he could take so much enthusiasm so early in the morning. "Wait a second. Just wait one second. Aren't you forgetting one important thing?" he asked. He sat up in Nick's lower bunk bed, being careful not to bump his head.

Nick looked himself up and down. "Let's see. I've got my Ray-Bans on, my suntan lotion on, my after-shave lotion on, my new aqua OP T-shirt on, my aqua-and-yellow board shorts on, and my tan boat shoes on," he said. "As far as I can tell, I haven't forgotten anything."

"It's not what you're wearing, stupid—it's what I promised your mother last night. Actually, I also made the same promise to myself."

"What was that?" Nick asked, playing dumb.

"That I'd look for a job today."

"Testing. I was just testing," Nick teased. "I wanted to see if you would stick to your guns."

"Believe me, I wish I could spend the whole day with you guys," Fury sighed.

"It's nine o'clock. My folks have already left

for work, so help yourself to breakfast. I'll see you later. Hi ho, hi ho, it's off to work I go," Nick sang, picking up his new, fiberglass short board and heading out the door.

Fury got out of bed, showered, and got dressed in his best pair of jeans, a button-down shirt, and his good jean jacket. Then he combed his hair a little more conservatively, to the side, instead of spiking it. The salt water yesterday had washed out almost all of the pink rinse and the shower he'd just taken had completed the job. Fury thought it was just as well that he looked a little less punk to go job hunting. It also crossed his mind that if he and Tracy ever got back together again, she'd be happy that the pink color had washed out.

After sprucing up, he felt hungry, but also a little strange about just helping himself to breakfast. He decided to get something to eat outside. But he did want to call Jed before he left Nick's house. He picked up the phone in Nick's room and dialed Russ's number.

"Hi, Jed," he said when someone picked up the phone.

"No, it's Russ. Who's this?"

"Uh . . ." Fury considered hanging up for a second. "It's Fury," he finally said.

"Oh. I'll get Jed. Hold on," Russ said brusquely.

"It's Fury," Fury heard Russ say to Jed. They were probably in the kitchen, Fury thought, having breakfast together.

"Hi, Fury. What's up?" Jed asked when he got on the line.

"Hey, Jed. I'm glad I caught you before you left to take care of Alex. I wanted to tell you that I'm not staying at the campground. Things didn't work out between me and Rain."

"Where are you now?"

"I'm staying at Nick's house."

"Thanks for calling and telling me. What else is new?"

"Well, I'm planning on looking for a job today."

"Hey, that's great! Good luck," Jed said.

"Yeah. Thanks, Jed. Listen, I was wondering if you could do something for me."

"Sure. Shoot."

"If you get a chance before you leave this morning, just drop the news to Tracy that I'm staying with Nick."

"You got it. Anything else?"

"Not now. But I'll keep in touch."

"Let me know if you find a job."

"I promise you'll be the first to know. Talk to you soon."

Fury hung up the phone. He took his Walkman out of his pack, slipped it into his jean-jacket pocket, and then flipped his skateboard into his hands with his foot. He was ready to roll.

As he pumped down the front path on his skateboard, he felt as fresh as the new white paint on Nick's house. He attributed the feeling to the shower, the first one he'd had in a few

days, and to wearing clean clothes. But something inside him made him feel just as good; as
much as he hated to admit it, he was actually
glad he was job-hunting.

Nick lived two blocks away from the beach,
just off Windward Way. Fury decided he'd stop at
one of the junk-food places on Windward for a
fast protein fix—egg, ham, and cheese on an
english muffin, and a cup of coffee. While he was
there, he could check to see if there were any
jobs available.

He skated through the golden arches, did a
couple of 180s in the parking lot, then zoomed
right up to the drive-thru window and ordered
his breakfast while standing on his board. He
skated into a parking place and ate his food, still
standing on his board. When he was done, he
tossed his sack of littler into a basket, gave
himself two points for the shot, then hopped off
his board and headed inside to check on a job.

He was back outside in two minutes flat,
having learned that the management wasn't
taking any more applications at the moment; if
he wanted to work for them, he'd have to come
back at the end of the summer. He skated down
fast-food row looking for work—and heard the
same story at all the fast-food chains. They had
done all their hiring at the beginning of the
summer.

Fury wondered whether he should try the
shops along the pier, or along Surfrider, next.
Since it was illegal to skateboard on the pier, he

opted for Surfrider. He skated from shop to shop looking for Help Wanted signs in the window. When he didn't spot any signs posted, he decided to make some inquiries on his own anyway—it couldn't hurt.

He skated up to the pharmacy, thinking that he might be able to use his experience as a messenger boy and land himself a delivery job. He hopped off his skateboard, picked it up, and confidently strode inside and up to the counter.

"Can I help you?" asked an older man in a starched, white jacket with short sleeves and a high collar. He capped a plastic bottle he had just filled with little pills and set it down on the counter.

"Yes, sir," Fury answered. "I was wondering if you need anyone to deliver prescriptions."

The pharmacist paused before answering. From behind a pair of bifocals, he gave Fury the once-over. Fury tried to stand up straight and look professional. Suddenly he knew what the pharmacist was staring at—he had forgotten to take out his red earrings. He blushed, hoping feebly that the earrings might blend in with the color of his face.

The pharmacist scowled. "Sorry. We don't need anyone right now. But, uh, thank you for dropping in," the pharmacist replied. He went back to work on his prescriptions.

Fury decided to head next door to Front Row Video. Before going in, he removed his earrings. When he walked into the store, he immediately spotted an employee with two earrings in one ear working behind the counter. Fury just couldn't win!

"Hey, man. I was wondering if you needed any help around here," Fury said.

"Not as of now, but we might in a couple of weeks. Want to fill out an application?" the man asked him.

"Sure," Fury said, feeling a little hopeful for the first time all day.

The man handed him an application and a pen. Fury filled it out as best he could, then handed it back to him.

"You left out your permanent address," the guy pointed out.

"I don't have one." Fury shrugged.

"Well, where could we reach you if a job becomes available?"

"I'm not sure," Fury said. "How about I just drop in again next week and check on the situation?"

"You can if you want, but if a job opens up, we'll have to fill it as soon as possible."

"I guess I'll have to take my chances. Thanks. By the way, do you have the movie *The Boy With Green Hair*?"

The man flipped through his rolling file. "We do have it, but it's checked out. It's been pretty popular this summer."

"Thanks," Fury said. He walked back outside.

He found himself standing right in front of T-Shirts For Two. Thinking about taking his chances, he decided to take another one. He walked into the shirt store and right up to the counter. He had no intention of asking Tracy for a job, but he was dying to talk to her and to tell her that he was at least *looking* for one. He waited for her to finish putting away a yellow "Here Today, Gone to Maui" T-shirt before getting her attention.

"Did Jed give you my message?" he asked when she was done with the task.

Tracy looked up, a startled expression on her face. Fury could tell that she had immediately recognized his voice, but was surprised to hear it.

"The pink's gone from your hair. And it's combed differently. It looks nice, but I liked it better combed the other way. The spikes are more you."

Fury got the feeling that Tracy was going out of her way to say something nice about his hair. Even though it was a little of a left-handed compliment, he still appreciated the effort. She seemed as if she didn't know what else to talk about.

"Your hair looks nice, too. It looks real full, like you just washed it," he told her. In fact, it looked so soft that he wanted to reach across the counter and touch it.

"I did. Now about the message," she continued, not dwelling on the compliment. "Jed told me this morning that you're staying with

Nick. I'm glad you found a place. What else is new?"

Fury got the impression that Tracy was trying to start a real conversation. It was nice. "I'm looking for a job today. I was just passing by so I thought I'd come in and say hello," he replied.

"That's great! Have you found one?"

"Not yet. And I probably won't if I stand here talking to you all day, so I should get going pretty soon."

"Well, good luck. I hope you land one."

"Thanks. Me, too." Fury was about to leave, but he still had something on his mind. "When will you be singing at the Surfrider?" he asked, dying to know how things had worked out with Will.

"I'm not. When Will decided not to headline me, I told him I wasn't interested in singing at Nashville Night."

"Oh, that's too bad. Look, I'm sorry. It was all my fault. I was way out of line with Will."

"Well, this may come as a big surprise to you, but you weren't as out of line as you may think," Tracy admitted. "Will wasn't being totally honest with me. He told me later that he had felt uneasy about headlining me all along. The truth was, he didn't think I had a big enough name."

"You should have told Will to use your middle name, too. Then your name would have been big enough," he joked.

"You know I don't have one," Tracy reminded him.

"Okay, then I'll make one up for you. Let's see. How about Tracy Charlotte-Mae Berberian?" Fury stretched out his arms in a dramatic gesture as he said the name. "I can see it now, spelled out in lights."

Tracy burst out laughing, and Fury giggled along with her. It felt so good to be with her again. He thought about his short but not sweet experience with Rain. "Over the last few days I've done some thinking, Tracy," he began. "And what I realized was that there's no one else in the whole wide world I'd rather be with than you. I'm sorry if I said or did anything to hurt you."

"Thanks, Fury. It means a lot to me to hear you say that. But you're not the only one who should apologize. If I hadn't said what I did at the house meeting, you wouldn't have had to move out. I really did you in that night. But you have to admit that you accused me of some pretty awful things," she pointed out.

"I admit it," Fury said softly.

"I know that when you saw me with Will the other morning—when I told you I would be at work—it led you to believe that there was something going on between us," Tracy continued. "But I want you to know that there was never *anything* but business between us. Now, what about you and that girl?"

"What girl?" Tracy's question caught Fury off guard.

"The one who drove you back to the house."

"Oh, *that* girl. Rain. I met her on the beach and spent the night with her," he blurted out. "No, no. That's not I meant to say. That came out all wrong. Let me explain."

"You'd better!" Tracy exploded.

"Okay. It's true that I met her on the beach and spent the night with her in her camper. But I was upset and drunk and I had no place to stay. So when she asked me if I wanted to crash in her camper, I must have said yes. The next morning, when I woke up, I didn't even know where I was. That was it. Nothing happened between us. And the next day I collected my stuff and moved in with Nick." As Fury related his story, he was relieved that things had actually worked out the way he was telling them. Tracy, Fury could tell, looked equally relieved. "So, now that we've cleared the air, what do you say we kiss and make up?" he asked, thinking that Tracy might just be receptive to the idea.

"Hey, not so fast. I don't know if I'm ready to do that just yet. How about we shake hands and try being friends for a while?" Tracy proposed.

"You've got a deal. Let's shake on it," Fury said. Tracy put out her hand and they shook hands for a minute. They might have stood there holding hands all morning if a customer hadn't walked into the store.

Fury dropped Tracy's hand. "I'd better go," he said.

Tracy nodded in agreement and busied herself folding a couple of T-shirts. She was back to being businesslike again, just the way she had been when Fury came into the store earlier. He waved good-bye and walked out the door.

As Fury skated down Surfrider toward the pier, he thought about his new relationship with Tracy. A real friendship based on mutual trust between them was evolving. He especially liked the way they had been totally honest with each other. In the long run, he now realized, this kind of relationship would actually be more secure than their old, hot-one-day, cold-the-next romance. Now that he thought about it, he really liked the idea of having Tracy as a friend. Better yet, he wanted to show her that he could be one, too.

Out of the corner of his eye, Fury caught a police car cruising by and jumped off his skateboard. He took his Walkman out of his pocket, put his earphones on, and walked the rest of the way to the foot of the pier. He ambled down it, listening to tunes and checking in shop windows for Help Wanted signs along the way. He even asked about a job at a seafood cocktail stand and a fish-and-chips take-out bar. But still he turned up nothing.

Fury was about to call it quits for the day and go sit in the sun when he spotted a sign: *Dishwasher wanted, eves., apply in person,* in the window of *Ports of Call* on the Pier. The job sounded perfect; he'd still have his days to go surfing. Fury took off his Walkman and earphones, stuffed them back in his jean-jacket pocket, crossed his fingers, and walked inside the trendy restaurant.

"We're not open for another hour," a man with a manicured mustache greeted him from behind the cash register.

"I'm not here to eat. I'm interested in the dishwasher job."

"Great. Do you have any experience?" the man asked, twirling one end of his mustache into a curl.

"If you mean can I wash dishes, sure."

"What's your name?"

"Angelo DeFurie."

"Nice to meet you. I'm Leonardo Donatello, the owner. The job pays five dollars an hour. If you want it, you're hired. I need someone to start tonight."

"You can take your sign out of the window. I'll take it," Fury said enthusiastically.

Mr. Donatello extended his hand. "I'll need you to start at six o'clock," the owner said, walking over to the window and removing the help-wanted sign.

"I'll see you at six, Mr. Donatello," Fury said on his way out.

"You can call me Lenny, Angelo."

"And you can call me Fury! I'll see you at six, Lenny," he said and skipped out the door.

"Way to go," Fury said to himself, making a fist and throwing his arm up in the air. He was talking to Tracy again and he had landed a job.

He wanted to race up to T-Shirts For Two and

tell Tracy the good news, but he had promised Jed that he'd be the first to know. And Tracy would find out soon enough from him. It was just as well not to rush things with Tracy.

The business of the day completed, Fury thought about hitching a ride to Zuma Beach to meet up with Nick and Danny. But Zuma was a good hour down the coast, and they might run into heavy traffic on the way back. Lenny seemed like he'd be an understanding boss, but Fury didn't want to risk being late on the first day of his new job. Now that life was on the upswing, he wanted to keep it that way.

Chapter 13

By the time Fury got back to Nick's house, changed into something more suitable for scrubbing pots and pans, and went out again to grab a roast-beef sandwich at the deli, it was already four o'clock. It was just as well, he realized, that he had changed his mind about heading down to Zuma. The day had disappeared.

As he sat down for his late lunch, Fury saw Leslie in the booth behind him, obviously on her afternoon break. He was happy to see that Jeff had hired a replacement for him. Fury considered talking to Leslie, mainly to brag to her about his new job, but remembered he'd promised Jed that he'd be first to know.

Leslie, it seemed, had no qualms about talk-

ing to him, however. On her way out of the deli
she walked up to him. "How's it going?" she
asked.

"Okay. Better than okay, in fact," Fury was
glad to report. "How about you?"

"Well . . . Jeff just hired a new relief lifeguard, so I should be happy. But she's turning
out to be even flakier than you were, if you can
believe that. She only started today and she was
an hour late this morning. I don't think she'll last
long," Leslie predicted.

"She doesn't by any chance have straggly red
hair?" Fury asked.

"Yeah, she does. How did you know?"

"I met her on the beach once or twice. You're
right—she won't last long. How's everything
around the house?" Fury asked, anxious to
change the subject.

"Pretty quiet, actually, without you around. I
heard you're staying with Nick?"

"For a little while. But I really miss everybody
at the house." Leslie looked surprised by Fury's
comment, and he could hardly believe what he
just said, either. It was true, though.

Leslie smiled. "It's crazy the way things
worked out. I'm sorry I had to side with Russ,
but I was really caught in the middle." She
shrugged. "It's too bad you had to move."

"Hey, Leslie, you don't have to apologize. You
did the right thing. I understand perfectly where
Russ was coming from. And you know what? If

your brother hadn't gotten on my case, I would have never shaped up."

"That's big of you to admit, Fury. But if you want to know the truth, I think Russ misses having you around to yell at. For someone who claimed to need the rent money so badly, he hasn't even done anything about finding someone for your old room. And every night since you left, Tracy goes into the den when she gets home from work and just sits and mopes in the beanbag chair. Whoops—I wasn't supposed to tell you that," Leslie said.

"That's okay. I stopped in at T-Shirts For Two this morning and Tracy and I are talking again."

"Fury, that's great! Maybe you and Tracy and me and Jeff can double-date again sometime," Leslie suggested.

"Well, we're not exactly *dating* at the moment. Right now we're working on just being friends."

"I wouldn't mind it if we worked on that, too. No hard feelings, Fury?"

"No hard feelings, Leslie."

"I've got to go. But I'm glad we had a chance to talk. Come by and say hello while I'm on duty sometime," Leslie said, heading back to work.

Fury finished his sandwich, paid his bill, and left the deli soon after Leslie. He went straight to the phone booth outside to call Jed. Luckily, this time he answered the phone instead of Russ.

"Stevens residence."

"Hey, dude, guess who?"

"Fury! Did you get a job?" Jed asked, sounding excited.

"Yeah. I got one as a dishwasher at Ports of Call on the Pier. I start tonight. And that's not all the good news—Tracy and I made up. Well, sort of. We're talking, anyway."

"Way to go, Fury. That's great."

"Yeah. Thanks for delivering my message to her. I think it softened her up."

"Listen, I'd love to talk to you more, but I'm in the kitchen making dinner. I've got something cooking on the stove."

"That's okay. I'm calling from a phone booth and I don't have any more change. Oh, one more thing. I ran into Leslie. I made up with her, too."

"All right! You're cooking! Oh, no! So is my spaghetti sauce. Gotta go. Bye."

"Catch you later," Fury said, hanging up the phone. He still had some time to kill before he had to be at the restaurant so he walked to the end of the pier, where the fishing boats had just come in. He watched the fishermen clean their day's catch, hosing the fish down, tossing their entrails into the sea. Hungry sea gulls hovered on wind currents around the boats, squawking and trying to catch some dinner of their own.

He rooted for one undersized, gray-and-white gull that was at a disadvantage because of a mangled foot. Although its flight was impeded and it was harder for it to compete for food with the healthier, more aggressive birds, it managed to survive by catching what fell from the other gulls' beaks.

Fury knew why he felt for the crippled bird. Like the bird, he, too, had been disadvantaged, but he had somehow learned how to manage. But life, he had recently discovered, was more than just managing. In the past he had used people like Tracy and Leslie to help him get by, often taking more than he gave. Even still they were willing to forgive and forget. If he went on acting in the same selfish way, he wondered how long they would put up with him. He had to act more responsibly from now on so that he'd never have to find out. Their friendship meant too much to him. When the fishermen were through, the sea gulls flew off and Fury realized it was time for him to get to work.

Arriving a few minutes early, Fury had enough time to look around the place before announcing himself to Lenny, who was serving drinks behind the bar. The restaurant, he noticed, wasn't very crowded. There were only a few people in the cocktail lounge, but it was only a few minutes before six o'clock, which was early for dinner. The place was attractive enough, Fury thought, done all in natural pine with forest green tablecloths, peach napkins, and brass lamps on all the tables. Decorating the walls were symbols of the sea: portholes, anchors, ropes, nets, shells, and stuffed birds. At the far end of the restaurant was an expansive, floor-to-ceiling glass window. Lined against it were romantic tables for two with unobstructed views of the sky and ocean. The waiters were mostly standing around, all dressed up in peach-colored, button-down, long-sleeved shirts and thin green neckties to match the table settings. There was even a dance floor, and music videos were being shown on a big screen in the bar. *This place must be popular with the young executive set,* Fury thought. *Before long I'll be up to my elbows in pots and pans.*

"Hi, Lenny. Lead me to the sink," Fury said, rolling up his shirt-sleeves when he was done surveying the restaurant.

"Fury! Right this way." The owner stepped out from behind the bar and escorted him through two swinging doors into the kitchen in the back.

Although Fury had begun his new job with a good deal of energy and enthusiasm, he lost his pep as the evening dragged on. It was not from too much work that he began to feel listless and fatigued, but from the lack of it.

"Not too busy in the dishwasher department tonight," Fury mentioned to Lenny when he came into the kitchen. "Anything else I can do?"

"Monday nights are generally pretty slow. Why don't you take a break and have some dinner? I'll tell the chef to prepare something for you."

"I don't know about the food here, but the people are great. Thanks, Lenny," Fury said.

"Only the best for our new dishwasher. Dan,

prepare our Monday-night special, the salmon florentine, for him," Lenny told the chef.

Dan Chin, the Chinese-American chef, seemed delighted to have something to cook. In no time Fury was sitting down to a delicious fish-fillet dinner, complete with freshly sauteed vegetables and rice pilaf. After eating, Fury stepped through the swinging doors and into the cocktail lounge. As he quickly crossed the dance floor to the restroom, he was surprised to find that the lounge was completely dead—no one dancing, no one drinking, no one even in sight. He remembered what Lenny had said about Monday nights being slow. Maybe things would pick up later in the week. If not, he might be out of a job soon!

But when Fury came to work on Tuesday night, business was no better. He was glad Lenny was paying him by the hour and not by the number of pots and pans to scrub. The only way Fury could tell Tuesday night from Monday night was that the catch of the day on the menu was different. Around eight o'clock, about the same time as Monday night, Lenny came into the kitchen and told Dan to prepare the Tuesday-night special for Fury.

As Fury sat down to another gourmet dinner, this time stuffed trout almondine, Lenny complained to him, "What am I going to do? I don't know how I'll pay the help this week. But if I don't pay them, they'll leave, like the dishwasher before you did. What difference does it make?" Lenny asked himself, throwing up his hands in disgust. "If business continues to be this bad, I'll have no choice but to close the restaurant."

Just my luck, Fury thought. *I'll get paid in fish specials this week. No wonder Lenny was so quick to hire me.* "How long has it been this way?" Fury asked, wondering how long he'd have his job.

"About three weeks. But this week's the worst. I can count the number of customers I've had on two hands. The first two weeks after we opened, we were packed every night."

Fury didn't know that much about the restaurant business, but from living up north in San Francisco, he did know a little about the eating habits of the trendy crowd. They were like the saying on the shirt Tracy had put away on Monday morning, "Here Today, Gone to Maui," going from one new restaurant to another.

"I think I know what the problem is," Fury told Lenny as he polished off his fish. "The crowd you had at first has gone somewhere else, to a new restaurant in town, on the pier, down the coast, somewhere. But they'll grow tired of that place, too. What you need is something to draw the pack back." Fury looked at Dan. "A change of menu, maybe Tex-Mex, Cajun. Either that or change the decor. When the yuppies get wind that something is different, they'll flock back.

They just want to make sure they're doing the latest thing."

"What's wrong with fresh fruit? The food is delicious the way it is," Dan protested. Fury wiped his mouth with his napkin. He couldn't agree more with the chef.

"And the restaurant is beautiful. I just spent a fortune decorating it," Lenny lamented. Fury couldn't argue with Lenny, either. The restaurant was elegant.

"Then maybe what you need is some sort of advertising campaign," Fury suggested. "Something to draw people's attention to Ports of Call on the Pier again."

"I had big ads in all the papers for our grand opening," Lenny said. "I can't afford to do another big ad campaign, not now."

"I've got it!" Fury said. "I think I can help you out. Why don't we print up some handouts? They're cheap to produce. And I come even cheaper. I don't have that much to do during the day, and I could distribute them around town," Fury offered.

"That wouldn't hurt. In fact, that's a great idea. But where's the hook, the gimmick, the draw?"

"A gimmick. A gimmick," Fury said. He stood up and began to pace around the kitchen.

"How about a two-for-one coupon?" Dan put in.

"I don't know. I tend to think that tells the customers you're desperate."

"Well, aren't you, Lenny?" Fury remarked.

"Complimentary champagne?" Dan said, trying again.

"Same idea," Lenny said. "But you're on the right track. Keep thinking."

While Dan threw out a few more suggestions, Fury kept pacing. He wasn't coming up with much, but at least he was walking off the dinner.

"That's it! I think I've got it!" Fury suddenly shouted.

"What? What is it?" Lenny screamed.

"It's so simple. I can't believe I didn't think of it before. Entertainment! Live entertainment! You've got a cocktail lounge half the size of a football field. If you pack them in for the entertainment, they're bound to stay on for dinner," Fury pointed out.

"Brilliant. The idea is brilliant. I've been told that fish is brain food, but I didn't know it could work so fast. Brilliant, Fury. The idea is brilliant," Lenny kept repeating. He hugged Fury and gave him a kiss on both cheeks, Italian style. "Just one small question. Where are we getting this entertainment?"

Now came the hard sell, the buildup, the drum roll. Fury knew he had to pitch the idea just right. One false move and Lenny could nix it just as quickly as he had said no to Dan's ideas. Best to be vague—keep Lenny guessing.

"Don't worry, Lenny. I've got that covered. Can you meet me here before the restaurant opens for dinner? Like around five o'clock tomorrow night?"

"Sure. Why?" Lenny asked, looking at Fury curiously.

"Because that's when I'm showing up with the entertainment. Don't sweat it. I promise you— it'll be great!" Fury said, full of enthusiasm.

"Well . . ." Lenny paused. "Okay. I guess I'll just have to trust you."

—ask for whisky. Like grown-ups, all the
time," she said.

"She—how," Kate asked, "have a cig-
arette?"

"Come then when I'm standing in the
dark shivering knot, awake in their piece you
still because Fera said, half . . . sentiments.

I will . . ." Kate asked, Vicky I said 40
that have to meet you."

Chapter 14

As soon as Fury got off work, he raced to the end of the pier to a phone booth. He didn't care what time it was or whom he woke up. He had to talk to Tracy, tonight. He dialed Russ's number and heard the phone ring several times. Finally, after five rings, Leslie picked it up.

"Hello? Who is this?" she asked, sounding as if Fury had awakened her.

"Fury."

"Fury, isn't it a little late for you to be calling? What time is it, anyway?"

"Around midnight. I'm really sorry if I woke you up. Look, is Tracy there?"

"She's sleeping." Leslie yawned into the phone.

"Could you get her for me? It's important."

159

"Are you sure, Fury? You know how she likes her beauty sleep. She's a bear if she doesn't get it," Leslie reminded him.

"I know, but I've got to talk to her. If it wasn't so important, I wouldn't be calling this late, Leslie—honest."

"Hold on. I'll get her," Leslie said.

While Fury waited for Tracy to get on the phone, he stuck his head out of the stuffy phone booth for a breath of air. He'd been breathing the smell of fish all night in the kitchen. The sea air was bracing and refreshing and made him feel alert. He looked out beyond the black ocean and up at the night sky. It was clear, not a cloud in it, he noticed, and the stars and a sliver of moon sparkled against the dark blue background.

"Fury, do you know what time it is?" Tracy asked, startling him.

"Sure. It's after midnight. 'I go out walking after midnight out in the moonlight . . .'" Fury sang, singing one of Tracy's favorites into the phone.

"Would you stop that singing and tell me why you're calling so late?" she asked, sounding as irritated with Fury's voice as she was with having been awakened.

Fury wasn't put off by Tracy's annoyance. "Chill out, Tracy. I've got some incredible news, the kind you sing about, the kind that can't wait until tomorrow," he told her.

"It better be good," Tracy remarked.

"It's better than good, it's great! I've got you

an audition for a gig. All you need to do is bring your guitar with you to work on Wednesday and meet me at five o'clock at Ports of Call on the Pier."

"Wow! Fury, that's fantastic!" Tracy shouted into the phone. "How'd you do it? What should I wear? What should I sing?"

"Don't get hung up on details, Tracy. I'll tell you how I did it tomorrow. Just remember, whatever you wear, whatever you sing, you'll be sensational. So be there!"

"Thanks, Fury. I love . . ."—Tracy hesitated, then, completed the sentence—"what you've just done for me."

Fury didn't have to be a genius to fill in the missing word. He knew what Tracy had intended to say.

I love you, too, he thought to himself, then made the sound of a kiss into the phone. "Now go back to bed and sleep on that. I'll see you tomorrow night."

Fury hung up and walked out of the phone booth. Although it was long after midnight, he still felt wide awake; he had no need for sleep tonight. All he needed to live was Tracy. No, that wasn't true anymore, he realized, as he headed down the pier and back to Nick's house.

It was true that he needed Tracy's love and support to make him feel whole. But equally important, he could stand on his own two feet— and not just on a surfboard. There was more to his life, he now knew, than waking up and wondering which beach to surf. It felt good to be taking on responsibility, to be helping out Lenny with his business and Tracy with her career. He never thought he'd be the one to admit it, but what he liked best about his new life was that it had direction and purpose.

"The way you look in that outfit, you won't even have to sing a note. Lenny will love you," Fury told Tracy when they met in front of Ports of Call at five o'clock on Wednesday night. She was wearing her white satin cowgirl blouse, black leather pants, and white boots, the same outfit she had worn the day Fury had seen her with Will, with the addition of a black leather vest with fringes and a black Stetson hat.

"Just so you won't be insanely jealous again, I wore it for you, not Lenny," Tracy informed Fury, setting him straight on that score.

"Thanks. Let's go in."

"Wait just one second. I'd like to know what's going on first. How did I get this audition?"

Fury told Tracy how he had gotten a job as a dishwasher at Ports of Call only to find out that the restaurant was on the verge of folding. Then he explained how he had come up with the idea of bringing in live entertainment to save it from going under and how he had convinced his boss to listen to Tracy sing. "We'd better go in now. Lenny's waiting for us," Fury concluded.

They walked inside and into the cocktail

lounge. Lenny was sitting down at one of the tables.

"Lenny, I'd like you to meet the entertainment, Tracy Berberian. She'd like to audition for you. She's a country-western singer," Fury said as they walked up to the owner.

"In that getup, I didn't think she sang hard rock," Lenny said, laughing. "Nice to meet you, Tracy. I'm Leonardo Donatello, the owner. If you sing as good as you look, you're the solution to all my problems."

"She sings *better* than she looks," Fury said, winking at Tracy.

"I'm sure she does. So stop sounding like her manager and let's hear her," Lenny said, encouraging Tracy to sing.

Tracy took her guitar out of her case, tuned a few strings, and broke into a medley of Patsy Cline favorites. Fury carefully watched the expression on Lenny's face change from one of mere interest to unadulterated rapture. Even before she had hit her last note, Fury knew that Tracy had won Lenny over.

"She's perfect for the lounge!" Lenny said, applauding Tracy's performance.

"Thank you, Mr. Donatello. When would you like me to begin?" Tracy asked politely.

"Saturday night. What do you think, Fury?"

"Saturday night's great. That will give me time to print up the handouts and distribute them around town. I want Tracy to open to a full house," Fury said.

"That makes two of us," Lenny agreed. He smiled at Fury. "Before I forget, here's a fifty to cover your printing costs." Lenny handed Fury a fifty-dollar bill. "Now that we've got all the details ironed out, we'd better get to work."

"I don't want to sound rude, Lenny, but aren't you forgetting one other important thing?"

"Not that I can think of. Can you help me out a little, Fury?"

"Tracy's salary," Fury reminded him.

"We'll have to charge a cover fee—say, five dollars per person. And until I can get the restaurant back on its feet, Tracy and I will have to split the take after the show. How does that sound to you, Tracy?"

"That's fine, Mr. Donatello. But regardless of what I get paid, I sing under one condition," Tracy said.

Lenny looked puzzled. "What's that?"

"Fury plays backup bass for me, and I split *my* take with him."

Fury beamed at Tracy. Had they been alone he would have swooped her up in his arms and hugged her. From the way Tracy looked back lovingly at him, Fury had the feeling she wouldn't have minded.

"You drive a hard bargain, Miss Berberian. You don't find dishwashers like Fury every day," Lenny said, only half-kidding.

Tracy gave the owner a look that clearly told him this was an all-or-nothing deal.

"But for you," Lenny said, turning to Fury,

"the help-wanted sign goes back in the window tomorrow morning."

Thursday morning Fury woke up to yet another day of clear, sunny Southern California skies. Nick was already dressed in a shirt and board shorts and, Fury assumed, he was just about to take off to the beach with Danny.

"Danny and I are going down to Malibu today," Nick said, as if he had read Fury's mind. "Want to come with us?" he asked.

"I can't." Fury sat up in bed and rubbed his eyes, hoping to wake up quickly.

"C'mon, Fury. It's a great day out. Why don't you come along?"

"I've got work to do," Fury protested.

"Work, work, work. I can't believe it. You're turning into a workaholic."

"I'd rather be a workaholic than a surfaholic."

"Look who's talking! I thought you purposely took a night job so you could surf all day."

"I did. But today I've actually got something to do that's more important to me than going surfing."

"In that case, it must be pretty important," Nick commented, smiling.

"It is. I promised my boss I'd make up some flyers and pass them out for him. In fact, I was planning to ask you guys to give up one of your precious surfing days and help me out," Fury explained.

"I'd be glad to help you out. Which way did you come in?" Nick kidded.

"Oh, groan. I'm serious, Nick. You're looking at a new man, the kind who doesn't shirk responsibility but welcomes it," Fury said in a serious tone. "But why am I wasting my breath? What would you know about responsibility?"

"Double groan. C'mon, Fury, give me a break. When have *you* welcomed it?"

"Okay, so maybe I haven't exactly welcomed it. But at least I'm not running away from it anymore. If I don't help my boss publicize the restaurant, it's likely to fold. Then I'll be out of a job again." Fury filled Nick in on how he and Tracy were going to perform on Saturday night to help Lenny bring back the customers. "So, are you going to help or not?" he asked Nick when he finished the story.

"Now, *this* is exciting! This I can get behind. You didn't tell me that you and Tracy were breaking into the music scene. I thought I'd be handing out two-for-one dinner specials or something. What are you waiting for, Fury? Get out of bed and get dressed," Nick said obviously impressed.

Fury jumped out of bed and into his shorts, high-tops, and a T-shirt. He combed his hair for a few minutes, trying to get it to stand up right, until Nick yelled at him to get moving.

An hour later Nick, Danny, and Fury were on the street passing out eye-catching magenta-colored handbills that read:

PORTS OF CALL ON THE PIER
IS PROUD TO PRESENT
FRESH FROM FRESNO
TRACY BERBERIAN
SINGING YOUR
COUNTRY WESTERN FAVORITES
THIS SATURDAY NIGHT, SIX—MIDNIGHT
IN THE COCKTAIL LOUNGE
COVER CHARGE—FIVE DOLLARS

Fury left Danny and Nick to cover the corner themselves for a while. He took a stack of handbills, headed up to T-Shirts For Two with them, and left some with Tracy to hand out to her customers. Then he made tracks over to Leslie's lifeguard station.

"Hey, Leslie!" Fury called up to her. "Do you think you could do me a favor and distribute these flyers for me?" He reached up and handed her a bunch.

Leslie took them from him and looked over the flyers. "Fury, that's terrific! Tracy didn't tell me she was singing. Sure, I'll help you spread the word. How'd she get the gig?"

"Well, I had a little something to do with it," Fury said modestly. Then he told Leslie the story of how Lenny had hired him as a dishwasher, how the restaurant was going under, how Fury had gotten his boss to go along with the idea of Tracy singing on Saturday night, and how he had volunteered to help distribute flyers to publicize the restaurant and the performance.

"Fury, I can't believe you did all that for Tracy and your boss! You've really gotten your act together."

"And Tracy's, too," Fury quipped.

Leslie smiled. "Russ should have kicked you out sooner," she said.

"Yeah, I know. Don't forget to tell everyone in the house to come," he said as he was ready to go.

"Even Russ?"

"Sure. Why not?"

"I don't know if he'll want to," Leslie said honestly.

"Maybe he'll want to if you put in a good word for me," Fury hinted.

"Well, I'll try."

"That's all I can ask. Thanks, Leslie. I'd better get going. I've got places to go and people to see," Fury said confidently as he headed toward the pier.

"And flyers to give out!" Leslie called after him, waving her bunch in the air.

Fury's next stop was the restaurant itself, where he left another pile next to the cash register. That gave him another idea. On his way back, he made stops at all the shops on the pier and left handbills with the shopkeepers who were willing to distribute them. By the time he got back to Nick and Danny, he was out of flyers and they were down to their last hundred. Danny suggested that they tack some up on telephone poles. Fury went back to T-Shirts For

Two, borrowed a stapling gun from Tracy, then set Danny to work putting them up on the poles along Windward and Surfrider.

By midafternoon they had distributed all one thousand of their flyers. Since there was nothing more for him to do until Saturday, Fury didn't see any point in turning into a workaholic overnight. There was only one way to spend the rest of the day, Fury thought. Surfing! After all, he couldn't work *all* the time. . . .

Chapter 15

Eat your heart out, Will, Fury said to himself on Saturday night as a crowd filed into the restaurant at six o'clock. *Now tell Tracy her name isn't big enough!*

In her shiny, red satin western shirt, black leather pants, red cowboy boots, and black Stetson hat, there was no doubt in Fury's mind that Tracy was a star—and she looked every bit the part. In his new western shirt, jeans, and cowboy hat, Fury knew he didn't look too shabby himself. Tracy had thought that his spiked, platinum-blond punk hair wouldn't fly with the hard-core country-western crowd. So, yesterday afternoon, when Fury had stopped into T-Shirts For Two to show off his new duds, she had surprised him with a black Stetson hat of his own. The only part of his outfit that didn't quite match was his pink high-tops.

The day before, Leslie had told Fury that she, Pamela, and Jed were definitely coming. Anticipating a good turnout, Fury had made sure to reserve a table up front for them along with Nick and Danny.

As he stepped up to the microphone to introduce Tracy and looked out on a packed house, Fury was glad he had. There, right in front of him, just as he had expected, sat Jed, Nick, Danny, Leslie, and Pamela. But to his surprise Jeff and Russ were at the table as well. Out of the corner of his eye he spotted Lenny standing near the door. Lenny signalled for him to start the show.

"Ladies and gentlemen, friends and enemies," Fury began. "Excuse me, I didn't mean to say that," he apologized, but the whole table in front started laughing and Russ, Fury noticed, was laughing the hardest. He smiled at Russ and made a gesture for the audience to quiet down. "Ladies and gentlemen," he began again.

"Romans, countrymen," someone shouted out.

"Pipe down," someone else told the heckler.

"Ports of Call on the Pier is proud to present Tracy Berberian, a fresh new talent in town," Fury continued without any further interruption. "Backing her up on the bass will be yours truly. Now let's give Tracy a big hand!"

Tracy stepped out from behind the bar and

walked up to the microphone, amidst catcalls, whistles, shouts, and a round of applause. Fury and Tracy took a moment to tune their instruments.

Tracy strummed a few chords. "I'd like to start off with a medley of Patsy Cline favorites," she said. She warmed up the crowd with her rendition of "I Fall to Pieces," then went right into "Sweet Dreams," "Blue Moon of Kentucky," and "San Antonio Rose."

In the middle of their last song, "Walkin' After Midnight," Fury broke in and played a short solo. As they finished, the crowd went wild, asking for more.

"Bravo!" Jed shouted above the noise. "All right, Fury!"

"Way to go, Tracy!" Leslie called out.

"I'd like to sing a new song I've written," Tracy said introducing her encore. "It's called 'The Other Side of Fury.'"

"I don't know that one," Fury said.

The table in front burst out laughing again.

Tracy smiled at him and started to sing. Fury was so touched by the fact that Tracy had written a song for him, he could hardly concentrate on the words. He stared lovingly at her, mesmerized by her beautiful presence as she sang the last few lines: "He's shown me he does care, and that he wants to share. . . . So if I'm his judge and jury, I love the other side of Fury."

After Tracy had finished singing, Fury stepped up next to her and put his arm around her. Then they took their bows. When he looked up again, the audience was on its feet, clapping, stomping, howling for more.

Lenny came up to the mike and quieted everyone down by saying, "There will be a short break, and then these great performers will be back. In the meantime, the restaurant and bar are open for service, and there will be dancing in the lounge."

Fury watched the crowd's activities with great interest. A good number of people sifted into the dining room. Many just ordered drinks and sat around waiting for the dance music to start. There was little doubt in Fury's mind that the show had been a great success, for him, Tracy, and Ports of Call.

"Why don't you sit down and join us?" Russ asked Tracy and Fury. Jed got up and grabbed two chairs for them from a nearby table. Fury and Tracy sat down between Russ and Pamela.

"Okay, I guess you all know why I called this meeting," Russ said.

"What meeting? I don't know what you're talking about," Fury protested.

"You're not supposed to, dummy. It's a surprise." Tracy whispered.

"After I finally talked Russ into coming tonight, Tracy and I also talked him into taking a new house vote," Leslie informed Fury. "So why don't we do it now and get it over with? All those in favor of . . ."

Fury looked at Leslie in amazement. He had

asked her to put in a good word for him, but getting Russ to agree to taking a revote on his staying at the beach house was definitely beyond the call of duty!

"Wait a second. Wait just one second. Let's not rush into this," Russ broke in. "Before we vote, Fury has to agree to follow a few rules. Rule number one—no dishes in the kitchen sink." It was obvious to Fury that Russ, not Leslie, was running this meeting, even though she had engineered it.

"Hey, that's easy, Russ. What's washing a few dishes to a professional dishwasher?" Fury joked.

"Rule number two," Russ continued, without smiling. "No hair dyeing in the bathroom sink."

"Why would I want to do that?"

"Rule number three," Russ went on, ignoring Fury's interjection, "No clothes in the living room."

"What about surfboards?"

"You read my mind, Fury. I was just getting to that. Rule number four—no surfboards in the house."

"Ah, c'mon, Russ, that's harsh. Can I at least put it in the carport?"

"Okay, but just be careful not to touch *my* car," Leslie warned. "And last but not least, Rule number five—rent *must* be paid on time."

"Do you accept American Express?" Fury teased.

"Cash or money order only, please."

"No problem, Russ. You'll have the rent tonight, right after the next show. But if you want it sooner, I can ask Lenny for it now."

"That's okay, Fury. Later tonight is soon enough," Russ said. "Now let's vote. All those in favor of Fury moving back into the house, raise their hands."

All hands at the table went up—even Jeff's, Nick's, and Danny's.

Russ counted hands, including his own, and announced, "It's unanimous, Fury. I don't know why, but we all want you back—even the guys who don't live at the house."

"It was Tracy's song that convinced me," Danny joked.

"And my vote for Fury to move back into Russ's house means he's moving out of mine," Nick explained.

"Well, if you want to know the truth, Leslie twisted my arm," Jeff said.

"What about you people who live in the house?" Fury asked, going along with the routine.

"I was just going along with the crowd," Pamela said, shrugging.

"Without Fury to eat my food, I've been putting on weight," Jed admitted.

"What about you, Russ?" Fury asked. "Why did you vote for me to move back in?"

"Because I've been dying to borrow your pink high-tops!" Russ said.

Fury looked at Russ to see if he was serious.

"I'll trade you," he offered. "You can have my sneakers if I can borrow the Suzuki!"

Russ burst out laughing. "That'll be the day."

"Fury, I think you'd better settle for your old room," Tracy suggested. "Don't push your luck."

"Don't worry," Fury told everyone. "I won't!"

Here's a sneak preview of *Cool Breezes*, book number four in the continuing ENDLESS SUMMER series from Ivy Books.

"So, did he kiss you?" Stephanie asked.

Pamela didn't answer.

"C'mon, Pam, you promised to tell me everything."

Pamela had been planning to tell Stephanie about her date with Russ all along. In fact, she had been looking forward to it. Who else, she had realized as she drove over to Doug's house on Wednesday morning, did she have to talk to? She had hoped to develop a friendship with Leslie, but in the one or two opportunities she had had, Pamela had somehow managed to say all the wrong things to her. The rest of the time, especially since Pam had started working with Stephanie, she and Leslie were like ships passing in the night. Now, Pamela was thankful that someone was showing an interest in her life, but Stephanie's interest was getting just a little too personal.

"Look, Stephie," Pamela said gently, "I don't make a habit of kissing and telling." The truth was, although she wasn't going to admit it to a fourteen-year-old, she wasn't even in the habit of kissing. Sure, she'd had a few boyfriends in high school, but she hadn't really felt that much for any of them. For all she knew, if she and Stephanie got down to comparing notes in the kissing area, her student might even be able to teach *her* a few things. Pamela, however, had no intention of ever finding out.

"Okay, okay, I get the message," Stephanie said. "But what did you do? Did you have fun?"

"Sure, we had fun," Pamela replied. "A lot of fun. Russ packed a picnic supper, and we went down to the beach to watch the sun set."

"How romantic," Stephanie sighed.

Pamela thought of how Russ had put his arm around her as they sat on the sand and waited for the sun to set. But, to Pamela's relief, that was as far as things had gone. Even still, just sitting close together and watching the ocean *had* been romantic, Pamela now realized.

"What else did you do?" Stephanie persisted.

"Oh, we played Frisbee and a little volleyball,

went for a swim, that kind of stuff. C'mon, Steph, we'd better get down to work," Pamela said, halfheartedly picking up a notebook. To be honest, she was as unmotivated to teach French today as Stephanie appeared anxious to learn it. By the time she and Russ had gotten back to the house, it had been around ten o'clock. By then Pamela had been too tired to prepare a new lesson for Stephanie and, before going to bed, she had decided she'd just wing it. But having to come up with drills this morning was an incredibly difficult chore.

As it turned out, she and Stephanie weren't the only ones having trouble getting going. Doug stuck his head in the doorway and waved the script he was working on at them. "Hey, do you two have a minute? I'm completely blocked on this scene and I wondered if either of you girls had any ideas."

The minute Pamela saw Doug's fabulous-looking, tanned face again, she had plenty of ideas. It made perfect sense to her now why she hadn't wanted to get too involved with Russ yesterday. Suave, sexy Doug was a hard act to follow.

"Sure, Dad. Come on in," Stephanie answered immediately. She seemed to welcome the interruption even more than Pamela.

"Why don't we sit outside on the deck? It's so beautiful out that it's a shame to be in here. Maybe the fresh air will help me get the cobwebs out of my brain."

Pamela, whose brain was feeling equally fuzzy, was thrilled with Doug's suggestion. Stephanie didn't appear to need any further persuasion, either. The two of them followed Doug out to the same round table where he had served them lunch the day before yesterday. When they were all seated, Doug put his script on the table and began to read a few lines. "Okay," he interrupted himself, "here's where I'm stuck."

Pamela sighed quietly. Besides Doug's distinguished good looks, she was being mesmerized by the deep, resonant sound of his voice.

After Doug had read about a page, he looked up once more. "Now, this is the point where I'm having the most trouble. Any ideas where I can go from here?"

Pamela drew a blank, but that was par for the course whenever she was near Doug.

"How about sailing?" Stephanie offered.

"I don't think I follow you, Steph," Doug said, frowning. "The characters are lost in a South American jungle. They aren't anywhere near an ocean."

"I wasn't talking about the— I was talking about us."

Her father laughed. "Got any other, more pertinent ideas?" Stephanie shook her head and he turned to Pamela. "What about you, Pamela? Did you come up with anything?"

"Huh?" she asked, coming out of her trance.

Why, she wondered, did Doug have this effect on her?

"I guess not." Doug paused and looked out at the clear blue water and equally clear sky above. "Stephanie's right. We *should* go sailing. Let's forget about trying to work today. On a gorgeous day like this . . . What do you think, girls? Could you take a day off from studying French?"

That was all Pamela and Stephanie needed to hear. Pamela had no second thoughts about bidding *au revoir* to French for the day and *bonjour* to Doug's thirty-foot sailboat, *Windansea*.

"No problem, Dad," Stephanie said with a whoop.

"I second the motion," Pamela said, only slightly less enthusiastically. She'd only been sailing once before in her life, and the prospect of going again was almost as thrilling as getting to spend more time with Doug.

"Well, in that case, I'll put this script away and meet you two down at the dock in about two minutes."

Pamela, on a hunch that today might be the day Doug would suggest that they go sailing, had dressed appropriately this morning. She was wearing a striped, blue-and-white tank top, jeans, her white Keds, and had tied back her hair with a blue bandanna. Stephanie had been wearing the same faded Levis and beat-up sneakers three days running, and her father, in his khaki shorts, thongs, and a red Ralph Lauren shirt, looked ready to go sailing at the drop of a hat.

Doug met the girls down on the dock where the boat was tied up, and once he and Stephanie had climbed aboard and unrolled the sails, he started barking strange-sounding orders to his daughter. Pamela knew that the most helpful thing she could do was to stay out of their way.

Finally, Doug and Stephanie had finished rigging the sails, put on their life jackets, and were ready to cast off from the dock.

"We almost sailed off without you," Doug said with a smile, extending a hand to Pamela.

Pamela shivered at his touch, and he looked at her questioningly. "Are you all right?" he asked, sounding concerned.

"Oh, I'm fine," Pamela assured him, willing her knees not to buckle as she stared into Doug's handsome, craggy face. "Things couldn't be better, really."